Major Contributors to Social Science Series

ALFRED MC CLUNG LEE, General Editor

Emile Durkheim

GEORGE SIMPSON

*Brooklyn College of the City
University of New York*

THOMAS Y. CROWELL COMPANY

New York, Established 1834

The selections in this volume have been taken from the following
editions of the works of Emile Durkheim. Specific page references
are given at the foot of the page on which a selection begins.

Division of Labor in Society, trans. George Simpson (Glencoe, Ill.,
1947). Reprinted with the permission of The Free Press. Copyright
1933 by The Macmillan Company.

Education and Sociology, trans. and introd. Sherwood D. Fox (Glencoe, Ill., 1956). Copyright 1956 by The Free Press, a corporation,
and reprinted with their permission.

The Elementary Forms of Religious Life, trans. Joseph Ward Swain
(Glencoe, Ill., 1948). Reprinted with permission of The Free Press
and Allen & Unwin Ltd.

Montesquieu and Rousseau: Forerunners of Sociology, trans. Ralph
Mannheim, ed. Alvin W. Gouldner (Ann Arbor: University of
Michigan Press, 1960).

Professional Ethics and Civic Morals, trans. Cornelia Brookfield (London: Routledge & Kegan Paul Ltd.).

The Rules of Sociological Method, trans. Sarah A. Solovay and John H. Mueller, ed. George E. G. Catlin (Glencoe, Ill., 1950). Eighth edition copyright 1938 by the University of Chicago.

Socialism and Saint-Simon, trans. Charlotte Sandler, ed. Alvin W. Gouldner (Yellow Springs, Ohio: The Antioch Press, 1958).

Sociology and Philosophy, trans. D. F. Pocock, introd. J. G. Peristiany (Glencoe, Ill., 1953). Reprinted with permission of The Free Press and George Allen & Unwin Ltd.

Suicide, trans. John A. Spaulding and George Simpson, ed. and introd. George Simpson (Glencoe, Ill., 1951). Copyright 1951 by The Free Press and reprinted with their permission.

To Louis and Jeanne Lister

Editor's Foreword

Undergraduates often find a great challenge in reading a seminal thinker's major contributions to social science in their original form. But students are usually offered either volume-length works containing stimulating passages embedded in outworn discussions, or brief excerpts included with those of other authors in general collections of readings. The longer works tend to be repetitious and wordy, and some now appear misguided. At the same time, excerpts in general collections do not give enough of a contributor's work to make him come alive.

In planning the present series, John T. Hawes, Director of the College Department of the Thomas Y. Crowell Company, and I sought manuscripts free from either of the above weaknesses. The editors were asked to dig out the main lines of a contributor's method and thought from the verbiage and the dated materials obscuring them, and to make available, in one slim volume, a critical essay together with the most significant and interesting passages in a contributor's writings. The volumes in the series, considered as a whole, thus give the student an understanding of the diverse ways of thought that have gone into the making of the social science discipline as we now know it.

The series has been edited and written so that each little book can be read for its own merits and without need of additional props. Each contains the seminal ideas of an author which still remain alive today but does not gloss over his weaknesses. Each book provides a critical vignette of the social scientist as he is now seen. Each book, too, should be interesting to college sophomores and especially to undergraduate majors in the various social sciences.

What all volumes in the series have in common is an educative conception. They are all efforts to interest undergraduates in some of

vii

the great "originals" of social science and thus to stimulate further exploration of important ideas and methods. The editor-critic who has done each volume has been free to follow his own professional judgment in analyzing his major contributor and in selecting significant excerpts from his works. Each volume thus has an individuality deriving from its editor-critic as well as from its subject.

The books in this series are intended to enrich introductory courses in the various social sciences. For more advanced courses, they will permit the student to become acquainted with the meatiest contributions of many selected social scientists rather than the few whose works he might read more extensively. Advanced students will find these books invaluable for the purposes of review.

ALFRED MC CLUNG LEE

Preface

The appearance in recent years of English translations of the bulk of Emile Durkheim's sociological work has made possible this compilation of readings.* My contribution here consists of a short introduction to the collection and commentaries at the beginning of each of its eleven sections.

Durkheim was preeminently a moral philosopher who used sociology as the scientific corpus for his attempt to establish moral philosophy on firm foundations. To portray him as the father of the arid "functionalism" found in the works of Talcott Parsons and Robert K. Merton is a disservice and a flight from moral philosophy. This functionalism emphasizes but a single aspect of Durkheim's thought and, in my opinion, not the most important one. Nor is Durkheim properly appreciated by making a cliché of his concept of "anomy." This book of readings, which includes his own words on anomy and selections from his sociological works generally, may help to cut through this and other clichés regarding Durkheim to reveal what he was trying to get at. What a thinker said and what his too ardent followers say he meant not uncommonly turn out to be different things.

G. S.

New York City
January, 1963

* The translation of *Division of Labor in Society* that I made in my salad days is inadequate. With the aid of Louis Lister I have completely redone the portions of that book reprinted here in sections 4, 6, and 11. Nevertheless, I have been troubled to find a satisfactory English translation for the French word *conscience*. *Consciousness* in English is awkward, especially in the plural, and not quite encompassing; *conscience* has ethical implications in English that go somewhat beyond Durkheim's French; *understanding* is too tame and impossible in the plural; *mind* is too substantival. With this caution to the reader, I have left it translated as *conscience*.

Contents

Introduction

Emile Durkheim has a secure place in the history of sociology, even though he has been the unfortunate victim of hero-worship and personal cultism in certain sociological circles in France and in the United States. Born in Epinal in the province of Lorraine in France in mid-April 1858, he was rigorously educated in lower schools there, at a lyceum in Paris, and then at the Ecole Normale Supérieure in Paris. The rabbinate had been the calling of the famous Jewish family Durkheim in France; Durkheim's father himself was an eminent one. From Judaic family training and an intimate environment Durkheim gained a deep and permanent concern for universal moral law and the problems of ethics, a concern that was not combined with any indulgent strain of humor. Indeed, he was eminently without humor and somewhat heavy-handed, traits redeemed by his overpowering dedication to sociology and by his vast learning.

At the Ecole, Durkheim came under the influence of Emile Boutroux, the philosopher, from whom he learned to think of society as a separate field of investigation, distinct from individual psychology and biology and not reducible to them. In that institution, Durkheim also came upon the writings of Charles Renouvier, a thinker in line with the German idealist philosopher, Immanuel Kant. Here also Durkheim was first attracted to the writings of Auguste Comte, the so-called father of sociology who had coined the word itself to describe the new science on which he saw humanity's hopes for the future resting.

Upon his graduation from the Ecole, Durkheim taught at lyceums in France until 1887, with one year (1885–86) off for study of higher education and sociology in Germany. There he became influenced by the evolutionary thinking of Spencer, Schaeffle, and Espinas, all three

1

of whom he used later in his first major work in sociology on the division of labor in society. In Germany he also came under the influence of the well-known psychologist Wilhelm Wundt.

In 1887 Durkheim gained a teaching post at the University of Bordeaux where he gave the first course in sociology in France, a subject at that time frowned upon by the older entrenched disciplines. At the age of thirty-five, Durkheim took his doctor's degree at the University of Paris (the Sorbonne) with a dissertation on the division of labor in society and a required thesis in Latin, which he wrote on Montesquieu. He had no easy time passing his doctor's examination, coming in conflict with the staid, conservative academicians by presenting an important and therefore controversial dissertation. But he did pass and was now formally qualified to hold a professorship. His substantive qualifications included literacy in Hebrew, Greek, Latin, German, French, and English, and a command of philosophy, psychology, biology, anthropology, sociology, economics, political science, law, religion, literature, art, education and pedagogy.

In 1896, as Dr. Durkheim he was appointed a professor of social science at the University of Bordeaux, the first chair in the subject in France. Finally, in 1902 he received an appointment at the University of Paris as professor of the science of education; it was not until 1913 that the title of his professorship at Paris became "the science of education and sociology." He died in 1917, leaving behind disciples in France and abroad who constituted a "Durkheim school of sociology."

Durkheim's life work in sociology is like a reflecting mirror of the issues, disputes, and problems of his times. The course of social evolution, the scientific status of sociology, the methods of social research, the need for specific research rather than sweeping generalizations, the relation of values to sociology, social aspects of economic life and of law, social control, solidarity, primitive and civilized mentality, the social characteristics of human knowledge, group psychology, the place of religion in human life, the discontents of civilization, new occupations and professional ethics, problems of education—these were among the topics to which he contributed.

Durkheim strongly held to the need for a collective psychology as the foundation for sociology and came to his now well-known doctrine of collective representations as the province of sociology in contrast with individual representations, the province of individual psychology. Collective representations for Durkheim proved to be handy fictional tools with which to attack the difficult study of the complicated relations among human beings. He could not foresee that one day we might be able to establish an individual psychology that would be inherently social. He aimed originally to prove that "society" had to exist in order for there to be a science of society. Yet in his study of religion, which was first published in 1912, he offers the view that religion fundamentally exists like society in the minds of individuals. But Talcott Parsons' statement, in his introductory remarks to the English translation of Durkheim's essays on education, that Durkheim must be credited with Freud for one of the most fundamental of all psychological discoveries—the internalization of culture in the structure of personality—is certainly stretching the point. Durkheim was unaware of the psychodynamics of the unconscious and of introjected imagery as systematically worked out by psychoanalysis, so that his conception of "internalization of culture" cannot be put in the same class as Freud's. Even so, some of Durkheim's psychological aperçus are exceedingly penetrating, especially since he did not know of Freud's work and that of the few other psychoanalytic theorists of his day.

Durkheim saw the science of sociology in two different ways, which sometimes complement each other and sometimes seem to oppose each other. On the one hand, he thought of it as progressing through individual pieces of research, such as his own work on suicide, and arriving at general social laws through such research. On the other hand, he saw it as a general science of society and societies considered from the point of view of social organization and social functions. "All that enters into their [societies'] constitution, or enters into the course of their development, is the sociologist's province." Rather than being one science among the several social sciences, "sociology can only be the system of the social sciences." We must note that much of what Durkheim claimed he derived empirically in his special research on suicide, he actually thought out inferentially through his vast knowledge and his remarkable ingenuity.

Durkheim claimed to be a positivist, but he was a peculiar type of positivist in conceiving of society as a collectively psychic phenomenon conveying moral obligations. It was mind that made society possible and morality that sustained it. Neither of these was materially reducible to biology or physiological psychology as it was for others who called themselves positivists. In his book The Rules of Sociological Method he sounds at times like an opponent of idealism: he would deal only with social facts rigorously defined; he would observe them without preconceptions and only secondarily with regard to individual manifestations; he would strive for statistical validation of theories. But the theories he tested in his works dealt with human emotions, human aspirations, human beliefs and thoughts, and not with their subsumption under reductionist philosophy as with some other leading positivists. Sociology, he tells us, can study morals and values objectively, but the sociologist is no moralist or value-propounder. In the still earlier book Division of Labor in Society, he had started to establish a science of morals objectively. But that a sociologist was for him fundamentally a moral philosopher as well as a scientist of moral behavior is already clear in that book when he discusses abnormal forms, dilettantism, and economic anomy. Certainly in Suicide his analysis of anomy is loaded with enlightening value-judgments. Despite these appraising value-judgments (indeed, perhaps because of them), Suicide can be looked upon as the first modern piece of distinguished, empirical, monographic research in sociology.

The concept of anomy, which Durkheim introduced into sociological thinking, is much bandied about today and has come to mean all things to all men. It is well to return once more (as in the readings in this book from Durkheim on anomy) to what he said, for what he said may not be the same as what some of his followers say he meant.

Onto the concept "society" Durkheim placed a very heavy burden. He saw society as a unity and at the same time as a seething cauldron of conflicting group aims and purposes in the modern world. He uses the concept to refer to the broad structure within which specific groups operate and also as a source of moral ideals for all groups and all men. Durkheim never made the distinction between "society" and "culture," the first being the structure of groups and relationships, the second referring to the codes of behavior and moral commandments. Hence, one of his contemporary British followers, Peristiany, claiming to follow in Durkheim's footsteps confusedly writes: "Even when individuals change their social environment they cling to the ideals of their society of origin as the main symbols of their social identity. This point is well borne out by recent studies of ethnic minorities in the United States." * This kind of terminological confusion is caused by using "society" in too many senses. Actually,

* Emile Durkheim, Sociology and Philosophy, trans. D. F. Pocock, introd. J. G. Peristiany (Glencoe, Ill.: Free Press, 1953).

what would be said today is that immigrant ethnic minorities in the United States have changed societies but have tended to carry their cultures with them.

Modern society as the center of a moral life is confounded by the conflicting moral codes of different groups within that society. Thus, there are professional groups whose moral codes are discordant with those of other groups or with general codes enshrined in law. Recognizing this discordance, Durkheim sought to offer the reform necessary to put an end to it. He thinks the way out of this moral dilemma is through the creation of professional or occupational groups which would become the basis of political representation and of the social structure in the future. We need, he writes, such groups intercalated between the State and individuals, groups that will restrain individual anomy and also protect the individual from an omnivorous State whose administrative organs and bureaucracy can swallow the individual and undermine the very democracy it is supposed to effectuate. But since Durkheim's day, the intercalated groups in Western society —industrial, business, labor, and professional—have themselves become bureaucracies.

Durkheim's conception of education as the process of leading the young into a moral and social life is categorical to the point of overlooking the conflicting moral aims of different groups in modern society. Through education, he holds that general social values may be implanted in the individual. He speaks of society here as an entity that educates towards its own ideals. Indeed, his notion of society as categorically applied to education can be used to oppose the very democratic pluralism he espouses in political life. In his personal life and in his public utterances on politics (as in the Dreyfus case, in which he was a leading academic figure in behalf of Dreyfus), Durkheim showed himself a thoroughgoing apostle of individualism and democracy, but some of his theoretical educational doctrines can be easily employed for quite opposite ends.

Sociology had begun as a highly secular science, even as an antireligious subject. Auguste Comte had seen society as evolving from the theological to the metaphysical to the positivist stage. In the last, the secular stage of positivism, the science of sociology would be the guideline for man's morality and his fundamental beliefs. But Durkheim found in his study of religion that religion responds to the needs of society and hence of individuals. From a study of primitive religion through the totemism of the Australian tribes, Durkheim concluded that religion in any given society consists of collective representations bearing upon the universal properties of things, of nature, and of people. Religion conceptualizes the world and the gods on the basis of the structure of the society itself. It is not from man's own nature that religious beliefs spring but from society, which determines man's nature. Anthropologists have severely criticized Durkheim's sociology of religion for resting on Australian totemism, holding that totemism is not universal and that some primitive societies are highly individualistic.

From his study of religion Durkheim arrives at a sociology of knowledge. He finds that conceptual knowledge consists of collective representations having their roots in society. Though not friendly to Karl Marx's views generally, Durkheim here owes an intellectual debt to Marx's and Engels' doctrine, "Social being determines social consciousness," and to their sociology of knowledge. But despite their foundation in society, the concepts of knowledge can come to lead an independent existence in interpreting objective knowledge, Durkheim tells us. The highest form of their independent existence is achieved in science.

Thus, wherever Durkheim looked—at economic life, at individual life, at education, at religion, at science, at morality, at work and play, at literature and art, at family life—he saw Society writ large. This single-minded commitment to what has been called "sociologism," backed by his massive learning, made the point of view he espoused unmistakable. Covering literately so many fields, he sounded like a veritable modern Aristotle, as one of his students at the Sorbonne in fact did call him. Even to those sociologists in Europe and in the United States who could not accept his particular brand of sociology, he stood as an overpowering figure in his devotion to their fast-growing discipline. In France during his lifetime he was sociology. Through his students at the Sorbonne he influenced the teaching and application of sociology throughout the country. He founded and helped to edit the periodical L'Année Sociologique, in which he often published articles and through which he exercised worldwide influence. Through his writings and lectures on education and pedagogy he left his mark on the school system and on university training in his native land. But the adulation his name inspires among his devotees Durkheim might find contrary to his views concerning the progress of science. What he said concerning his work on Suicide there is every reason for believing he held to concerning all his work: "There is nothing necessarily discouraging in the incompleteness of the results thus far obtained; they should arouse new efforts, not surrender. . . . This makes possible some continuity in scientific labor —continuity upon which progress depends."

Montesquieu as Forerunner of the Science of Sociology*

In the Latin thesis required for the doctor's degree at the Sorbonne, Durkheim wrote on Montesquieu's contribution to scientific thinking about society. Thus he was enabled to show a continuity of thinking along sociological lines that predated the invention of the word "sociology" by Auguste Comte, a demonstration that could aid in making the subject more palatable to the die-hard, tradition-bound academicians who opposed according it a formal place in French higher learning. Comte himself had words of praise for Montesquieu. In Montesquieu, Durkheim found support for his own search for types of society, which he pursued in his doctoral dissertation on the division of labor. Durkheim also found support in Montesquieu for his own attempt to discover laws of social development and of collective behavior.

Not only did Durkheim's view of Montesquieu as sociology's forerunner deepen the historical roots of the new discipline that Durkheim wished to have accepted into academic life; by linking it with an even earlier Frenchman than Comte, he was invoking patriotism to further sociology's cause in France. To deny a subject founded by eminent Frenchmen, which was already (in 1893) hailed and pursued by British and German thinkers, would in his view be unpardonable.

Unmindful of our history, we have fallen into the habit of regarding social science as foreign to our ways and to the French mind. The prestige of recent works on the subject by eminent English and Ger-

* From *Montesquieu and Rousseau: Forerunners of Sociology*, pp. 1–2, 61–64.

man philosophers has made us forget that this science came into being in our country. Not only was it a Frenchman, Auguste Comte, who laid its actual foundations, distinguished its essential parts and named it sociology—a rather barbarous name to tell the truth—but the very impetus of our present concern with social problems came from our eighteenth-century philosophers. In that brilliant group of writers, Montesquieu occupies a place apart. It was he, who, in *The Spirit of Laws*, laid down the principles of the new science.

To be sure, Montesquieu did not discuss all social phenomena in this work, but only one particular kind, namely laws. Nevertheless, his method of interpreting the various forms of law is also valid for other social institutions and can, generally speaking, be applied to them. As laws bear upon all of social life, he necessarily deals with almost all aspects of society. Thus, in order to explain the nature of domestic law, to show how laws harmonize with religion, morality, etc., he is obliged to investigate religion, morality and the family, with the result that he has actually written a treatise dealing with social phenomena as a whole.

By this I do not mean to say that Montesquieu's work contains very many propositions that modern science can accept as well-demonstrated theorems. Almost all the instruments we require for exploring the nature of societies were lacking in Montesquieu's time. Historical science was in its infancy and just beginning to develop; travelers' tales about faraway peoples were few and untrustworthy; statistics, which enables us to classify the various events of life (deaths, marriages, crimes, etc.) according to a definite method, was not yet in use. Furthermore, since society is a large living organism with a characteristic mind comparable to our own, a knowledge of the human mind and its laws helps us to perceive the laws of society more accurately. In the last century such studies were all in their barest beginnings. Still, the discovery of unquestionable truths is by no means the only way of contributing to science. It is equally important to make science aware of its subject matter, its nature and method, and to lay its groundwork. This was precisely what Montesquieu did for our science. He did not always interpret history correctly, and it is easy to prove him wrong. But no one before him had gone so far along the way that led his successors to true social science. No one had perceived so clearly the conditions necessary for the establishment of this discipline. . . .

. . . . . .

. . . . Although it is always a mistake to trace the birth of a science to a particular thinker—since every science is the product of an unbroken chain of contributions and it is hard to say exactly when it came into existence—nevertheless, it is Montesquieu who first laid down the fundamental principles of social science. Not that he stated them in explicit terms. He speculated very little about the conditions of the science he inaugurated. But these principles and conditions are inherent in his ideas, and it is not difficult to recognize and formulate them. . . .

. . . . Not only did Montesquieu understand that social phenomena are matter for scientific study; he also helped to shape the two fundamental ideas necessary for the establishment of social science, namely the ideas of *type* and of *law*.

In regard to *type*, Montesquieu shows that the nature of the sovereign power and of social existence in general differs from one society to another, but that the different forms can nevertheless be compared. This is an indispensable condition for classification; it is not enough that societies should manifest similarities of one kind or another; it must be possible to compare them in their whole structure and existence. Montesquieu not only formulated principles, but also used them with great skill. His rough classification contains a considerable element of truth. But he was mistaken in two points. First, he erroneously assumes that social forms are determined by the forms of sovereignty and can be defined accordingly. Second, he states that there is something intrinsically abnormal about one of the types he distinguishes, namely, the despotic state. Such a view is incompatible with the nature of a type, for each type has its own perfect form which—allowances being made for conditions of time and place— is equal in rank to the perfect form of the other types.

As for the notion of *law*, it was more difficult to transfer it from the other sciences in which it was already established to ours. In all sciences the notion of type appears earlier than that of law, because the human mind conceives it more readily. One has only to look around to note certain similarities and differences between things. But the determinate relations we call laws are closer to the nature of things and consequently hidden within it. They are covered by a veil that we must first remove if we are to get at them and bring them to light. In regard to social science, there were certain special difficulties resulting from the very nature of social existence, which is so mobile, diversified, and rich in forms that to my mind it cannot be reduced to fixed and immutable laws. Moreover, men do not like to think that they are bound by the same necessity as other natural phenomena.

Nevertheless, despite appearances, Montesquieu maintains that social phenomena have a fixed and necessary order. He denies that societies are organized haphazardly and that their history depends on accidents. He is convinced that this sphere of the universe is governed by laws, but his conception of them is confused. According to him, they do not tell us how the nature of a society gives rise to social institutions, but rather indicate the institutions that the nature of a society requires, as if their efficient cause were to be sought only in the will of the lawgiver. He also applies the word laws to relations between ideas rather than between things. To be sure these ideas are those which a society must hold if it is faithful to its nature, but it can depart from them. Yet his social science does not degenerate into pure dialectics because he realizes that what is rational is precisely what exists most often in reality. Thus his ideal logic is to some extent situated in the empirical world. But there are exceptions which introduce an element of ambiguity into his concept of law.

Since Montesquieu all social science has endeavored to dissipate this ambiguity. No further progress could be made until it was established that the laws of societies are no different from those governing the rest of nature and that the method by which they are discovered is identical with that of the other sciences. This was Auguste Comte's contribution. From the notion of law he eliminated all the foreign elements that had hitherto falsified it, and he rightly insisted on the primacy of the inductive method. Only then could our science become fully aware of its objective and method. Only then was its indispensable groundwork complete.

2

❧❧❧

Sociology, Collective Psychology, and the Reality of Society

In Auguste Comte's view, the positivist stage of society was the stage in which men sought for scientific answers to questions formerly answered by theology and metaphysics. For Durkheim, as for Comte, positivism was absolutely necessary to the development of sociology as a science. But to be able to study society scientifically, it must be shown to exist. If society consists only of individuals and their relationships, Durkheim saw sociology as a supernumerary in the hierarchy of sciences whose place could be adequately filled by individual psychology.

According to Durkheim, society exists as more than a conceptual fiction. Its existence, however, is of a different sort from the existence of individuals. There is a realm of ideas, of "representations" which are not originally in individuals but which individuals incorporate. These "collective representations," as Durkheim called them, are outside of individuals originally and exercise a sanctioning power over individual behavior. Individual psychology cannot study them with its tools of investigation; they must be studied by collective psychology, that is, by sociology.

Collective representations as methodological artifacts, as shorthand expressions for subsuming the complexities of relationships among individuals, may be given a central place in sociology as Durkheim wished. He did not, however, always look upon them as artifacts, as shorthand expressions, but on occasion treated them as real substances. This position was to cause him trouble all through his work. In the commentary introducing Chapter 9, more is said about this fallacy known as "hypostasis."

Positivism*

. . . . The most impressive event in the philosophic history of the nineteenth century was the founding of positive philosophy. In the presence of the increasing specialization of sciences and their increasingly positive nature, one might wonder whether humanity's early aspiration for unity of knowledge could henceforth be considered an illusion, a deceiving perspective, which it was necessary to renounce. One might fear consequently that the sciences, and thus their unity, were more and more fragmented. Positive philosophy was a reaction against this tendency, a protest against this renunciation. It asserts that the eternal ambition of the human mind has not lost all legitimacy, that the advance of the special sciences is not its negation, but that a new means must be employed to satisfy it. Philosophy, instead of seeking to go beyond the sciences, must assume the task of organizing them, and must organize them in accordance with their own method—by making itself positive. An entirely new vista was thus opened up for thought. This is why it can be said that, aside from Cartesianism, there is nothing more important in the entire history of French philosophy. And at more than one point these two philosophies can legitimately be reconciled with each other, for they were both inspired by the same rationalist faith. But . . . the idea, the word, and even the outline of positivist philosophy are all found in Saint-Simon. He was the first to conceive that between the formal generalities of metaphysical philosophy and the narrow specialization of the particular sciences, there was a place for a new enterprise, whose pattern he supplied and himself attempted. Therefore, it is to him that one must, in full justice, award the honor currently given Comte.

But this is not all. One of the great innovations positive philosophy brought along with it is positive sociology. As has been said, it is the integration of social science into the circle of the natural sciences. In this regard, one might say of positivism that it has enriched human intelligence, that it has created new horizons. To add a science to the list of sciences is always a very laborious operation, but more productive than the annexation of a new continent to old continents.

* From *Socialism and Saint-Simon*, pp. 104–5, 108.

And it is at once much more fruitful when the science has man for its object. It almost had to do violence to the human spirit and to triumph over the keenest resistance to make it understood that in order to act upon things it was first necessary to put them on trial. The resistance has been particularly stubborn when the material to be examined was ourselves, due to our tendency to place ourselves outside of things, to demand a place apart in the universe.

Saint-Simon was the first who resolutely freed himself from these prejudices. Although he may have had precursors, never had it been so clearly asserted that man and society could not be directed in their conduct unless one began by making them objects of science, and further that this science could not rest on any other principles than do the sciences of nature. And this new science—he not only laid out its design but attempted to realize it in part. We can see here all that Auguste Comte, and consequently all that the thinkers of the nineteenth century, owe him. In him we encounter the seeds already developed of all the ideas which have fed the thinking of our time. We have just found in it positivist philosophy, positivist sociology. . . .

. . . . .

. . . . What differentiates Comte and Saint-Simon is that the former separated science from practice more clearly, but without disinteresting himself in the latter—at least during the better part of his career. Once given this idea of a positive science of societies, he undertook to realize it, not from the aspect of this or that immediate end, but in an abstract and disinterested manner. Although he was always convinced that his theoretical works could and would finally have an effect on the course of events, he understood that before all else he had to produce a scholarly work, to pose the problems of science in all its generality. And although he expects, at the end of his studies, to find solutions applicable to the difficulties of the present time, he believes they must result from an established science, although not contesting these so-called ends as essential. Saint-Simon did not possess the same degree of scientific patience. A definite social crisis had stirred his thought, and it was entirely to solve it that all his efforts were bent. His entire system, consequently, has a practical—not a remote—objective which he hastens to attain, and he has science do nothing but approach this goal. Therefore, although he was the first to have a really clear conception of what sociology had to be and its necessity, strictly speaking, he did not create a sociology. He didn't use the method, whose principles he had so firmly stated, to discover the laws of evolution—social and general—but in order to answer a very special question—of entirely immediate interest—which can be formulated as follows: what is the social system required by the condition of European societies on the morrow of the Revolution?

Sociology and Society's Existence *

Sociology has been in vogue for some time. Today this word, little known and almost discredited a decade ago, is in common use. Representatives of the new science are increasing in number and there is something like a public feeling favorable to it. Much is expected of it. It must be confessed, however, that results up to the present time are not really proportionate to the number of publications nor the interest which they arouse. The progress of a science is proven by the progress toward solution of the problems it treats. It is said to be advancing when laws hitherto unknown are discovered, or when at least new facts are acquired modifying the formulation of these problems even though not furnishing a final solution. Unfortunately, there is good reason why sociology does not appear in this light, and this is because the problems it proposes are not usually clear-cut. It is still in the stage of system-building and philosophical syntheses. Instead of attempting to cast light on a limited portion of the social field, it prefers brilliant generalities reflecting all sorts of questions to definite treatment of any one. Such a method may indeed momentarily satisfy public curiosity by offering it so-called illumination on all sorts of subjects, but it can achieve nothing objective. Brief studies and hasty intuitions are not enough for the discovery of the laws of so complex a reality. And, above all, such large and abrupt generalizations are not capable of any sort of proof. All that is accomplished is the occasional citation of some favorable examples illustrative of the hypothesis considered, but an illustration is not a proof. Besides, when so many various matters are dealt with, none is competently treated and only casual sources can be employed, with no means to make a critical estimate of them. Works of pure sociology are accord ingly of little use to whoever insists on treating only definite ques

* From *Suicide*, pp. 35–36, 37–38.

tions, for most of them belong to no particular branch of research and in addition lack really authoritative documentation.

Believers in the future of the science must, of course, be anxious to put an end to this state of affairs. If it should continue, sociology would soon relapse into its old discredit and only the enemies of reason could rejoice at this. The human mind would suffer a grievous setback if this segment of reality which alone has so far denied or defied it should escape it even temporarily. There is nothing necessarily discouraging in the incompleteness of the results thus far obtained. They should arouse new efforts, not surrender. A science so recent cannot be criticized for errors and probings if it sees to it that their recurrence is avoided. Sociology should, then, renounce none of its aims; but, on the other hand, if it is to satisfy the hopes placed in it, it must try to become more than a new sort of philosophical literature. Instead of contenting himself with metaphysical reflection on social themes, the sociologist must take as the object of his research groups of facts clearly circumscribed, capable of ready definition, with definite limits, and adhere strictly to them. Such auxiliary subjects as history, ethnography and statistics are indispensable. The only danger is that their findings may never really be related to the subject he seeks to embrace; for, carefully as he may delimit this subject, it is so rich and varied that it contains inexhaustible and unsuspected tributary fields. But this is not conclusive. If he proceeds accordingly, even though his factual resources are incomplete and his formulae too narrow, he will have nevertheless performed a useful task for future continuation. Conceptions with some objective foundation are not restricted to the personality of their author. They have an impersonal quality which others may take up and pursue; they are transmissible. This makes possible some continuity in scientific labor—continuity upon which progress depends. . . .

. . . . .

Sociological method as we practice it rests wholly on the basic principle that social facts must be studied as things, that is, as realities external to the individual. There is no principle for which we have received more criticism; but none is more fundamental. Indubitably for sociology to be possible, it must above all have an object all its own. It must take cognizance of a reality which is not in the domain of other sciences. But if no reality exists outside of individual consciousness, it wholly lacks any material of its own. In that case, the only possible subject of observation is the mental states of the individual, since nothing else exists. That, however, is the field of psychology. From this point of view the essence of marriage, for example, or the family, or religion, consists of individual needs to which these institutions supposedly correspond: paternal affection, filial love, sexual desire, the so-called religious instinct, etc. These institutions themselves, with their varied and complex historical forms, become negligible and of little significance. Being superficial, contingent expressions of the general characteristics of the nature of the individual, they are but one of its aspects and call for no special investigation. Of course, it may occasionally be interesting to see how these eternal sentiments of humanity have been outwardly manifested at different times in history; but as all such manifestations are imperfect, not much importance may be attached to them. Indeed, in certain respects, they are better disregarded to permit more attention to the original source whence flows all their meaning and which they imperfectly reflect. On the pretext of giving the science a more solid foundation by establishing it upon the psychological constitution of the individual, it is thus robbed of the only object proper to it. *It is not realized that there can be no sociology unless societies exist, and that societies cannot exist if there are only individuals.* Moreover, this view is not the least of the causes which maintain the taste for vague generalities in sociology. How can it be important to define the concrete forms of social life, if they are thought to have only a borrowed existence?

Collective Representations
and Society's Existence*

When we said elsewhere that social facts are in a sense independent of individuals and exterior to individual minds, we only affirmed of the social world what we have . . . established for the psychic world. Society has for its substratum the mass of associated individuals. The system which they form by uniting together, and which varies according to their geographical disposition and the nature and number of their channels of communication, is the base from which social life

* From *Sociology and Philosophy*, pp. 24–26, 28–32, 34.

is raised. The representations which form the network of social life arise from the relations between the individuals thus combined or the secondary groups that are between the individuals and the total society. If there is nothing extraordinary in the fact that individual representations, produced by the action and reaction between neural elements, are not inherent in these elements, there is nothing surprising in the fact that collective representations, produced by the action and reaction between individual minds that form the society, do not derive directly from the latter and consequently surpass them. The conception of the relationship which unites the social substratum and the social life is at every point analogous to that which undeniably exists between the physiological substratum and the psychic life of individuals, if, that is, one is not going to deny the existence of psychology in the proper sense of the word. The same consequences should then follow on both sides. The independence, the relative externality of social facts in relation to individuals, is even more immediately apparent than is that of mental facts in relation to the cerebral cells, for the former, or at least the most important of them, bear the clear marks of their origin. While one might perhaps contest the statement that all social facts without exception impose themselves from without upon the individual, the doubt does not seem possible as regards religious beliefs and practices, the rules of morality and the innumerable precepts of law—that is to say, all the most characteristic manifestations of collective life. All are expressly obligatory, and this obligation is the proof that these ways of acting and thinking are not the work of the individual but come from a moral power above him, that which the mystic calls God or which can be more scientifically conceived. The same law is found at work in the two fields.

Furthermore, it can be explained in the same way in the two cases. If one can say that, to a certain extent, collective representations are exterior to individual minds, it means that they do not derive from them as such but from the association of minds, which is a very different thing. No doubt in the making of the whole each contributes his part, but private sentiments do not become social except by combination under the action of the *sui generis* forces developed in association. In such a combination, with the mutual alterations involved, *they become something else.* A chemical synthesis results which concentrates and unifies the synthesised elements and by that transforms them. Since this synthesis is the work of the whole, its sphere is the whole. The resultant surpasses the individual as the whole the part. It is *in* the whole as it is *by* the whole. In this sense it is exterior to the individuals. No doubt each individual contains a part, but the whole is found in no one. In order to understand it as it is one must take the aggregate in its totality into consideration. It is that which thinks, feels, wishes, even though it can neither wish, feel, nor act except through individual minds. We can see here also how it is that society does not depend upon the nature of the individual personality. In the fusion from which it results all the individual characteristics, by definition divergent, have neutralized each other. Only those more general properties of human nature survive, and precisely because of their extreme generality they cannot account for the specialized and complex forms which characterize collective facts. This is not to say that they count for nothing in the resultant, but they are only its mediate conditions. Without them it could not emerge, but they do not determine it.

. . . . .

Those, then, who accuse us of leaving social life in the air because we refuse to reduce it to the individual mind have not, perhaps, recognized all the consequences of their objection. If it were justified it would apply just as well to the relations between mind and brain, for in order to be logical they must reduce the mind to the cell and deny mental life all specificity. But then one falls into the dire difficulties that we have already indicated. Following the same principle, one would be bound to say that the properties of life consist in particles of oxygen, hydrogen, carbon and nitrogen, which compose the living protoplasm, since it contains nothing beyond these particular minerals just as society contains nothing more than the individuals.[1] Here the impossibility of the conception which we are opposing will perhaps appear with even greater clarity than in the earlier instances. How can living movements be based in non-living elements? How are the characteristic properties of life distributed among these elements? They cannot be equally divided since they are different. Oxygen cannot play the same role as carbon or be invested with the same properties. No less inadmissible is the contention that each aspect of life is embodied in a different group of atoms. Life cannot be thus divided; it is one, and consequently cannot be based on anything other than the living substance in its totality. It is in the whole, not in the parts.

[1] At least, individuals are the only active elements. More correctly, society also comprises things.

If, then, to understand it as it is, it is not necessary to disperse it among the elementary forces of which it is the resultant, why should it be different for the individual mind in relation to the cerebral cells and social facts in relation to individuals?

In fact individualistic sociology is only applying the old principles of materialist metaphysics to social life. It claims, that is, to explain the complex by the simple, the superior by the inferior, and the whole by the part, which is a contradiction in terms. The contrary principle does not seem to us to be any less questionable. One cannot, following idealist and theological metaphysics, derive the part from the whole, since the whole is nothing without the parts which form it and cannot draw its vital necessities from the void. We must, then, explain phenomena that are the product of the whole by the characteristic properties of the whole, the complex by the complex, social facts by society, vital and mental facts by the *sui generis* combinations from which they result. This is the only path that a science can follow. This is not to say that there is a solution of continuity between these various stages of reality. The whole is only formed by the grouping of the parts, and this grouping does not take place suddenly as a result of a miracle. There is an infinite series of intermediaries between the state of pure isolation and the completed state of association. But as the association is formed it gives birth to phenomena which do not derive directly from the nature of the associated elements, and the more elements involved and the more powerful their synthesis, then the more marked is this partial independence. No doubt it is this that accounts for the flexibility, freedom and contingence that the superior forms of reality show in comparison with the lower forms in which they are rooted. In fact, when a way of doing or being depends from a whole without depending immediately from the parts which compose that whole, it enjoys, as a result of this diffusion, a ubiquity which to a certain extent frees it. As it is not fixed to a particular point in space it is not bound by too narrowly limited conditions of existence. If some cause induces a variation, that variation will encounter less resistance and will come into existence more easily because it has, in a way, a greater scope for movement. If certain of the parts reject it, certain others will form the basis (*point d'appui*) necessary for the new arrangement without, for all that, being obliged to rearrange themselves. That at least is how one can conceive how it is that one organ is able to perform different functions, different parts of the brain can substitute for each other, and one social institution can successively further the most varied ends.

Also, while it is through the collective substratum that collective life is connected to the rest of the world, it is not absorbed in it. It is at the same time dependent on and distinct from it, as is the function of the organ. As it is born of the collective substratum the forms which it manifests at the time of its origin, and which are consequently fundamental, naturally bear the marks of their origin. For this reason the basic matter of the social consciousness is in close relation with the number of social elements and the way in which they are grouped and distributed, etc.—that is to say, with the nature of the substratum. But once a basic number of representations has been thus created, they become, for the reasons which we have explained, partially autonomous realities with their own way of life. They have the power to attract and repel each other and to form amongst themselves various syntheses, which are determined by their natural affinities and not by the condition of their matrix. As a consequence, the new representations born of these syntheses have the same nature; they are immediately caused by other collective representations and not by this or that characteristic of the social structure. The evolution of religion provides us with the most striking examples of this phenomenon. It is perhaps impossible to understand how the Greek or Roman Pantheon came into existence unless we go into the constitution of the city, the way in which the primitive clans slowly merged, the organization of the patriarchal family, etc. Nevertheless the luxuriant growth of myths and legends, theogonic and cosmological systems, etc., which grow out of religious thought, is not directly related to the particular features of the social morphology. Thus it is that the social nature of religion has been so often misunderstood.

It has been believed that it is formed to a great extent by extra-social forces because the immediate link between the greater part of religious beliefs and the organization of society has not been perceived. By this reasoning one would have to exclude from psychology everything beyond pure sensation. For if sensation, this primary store of the individual mind, cannot be explained except by the condition of the brain and the organs, once it exists it forms itself according to laws which neither morphology nor cerebral physiology can adequately account for. From this derive images and these, in their turn, group to form conceptions. As these new states are added to the old, as they are separated by more intermediaries from the organic base upon which, nevertheless, all mental life rests, they become less immediately dependent upon it. They do not cease to be psychic facts, for it is in them that one can best observe the characteristic attributes of the mind.

Perhaps these comparisons will make clear why we insist so much upon a distinction between sociology and individual psychology.

. . . . .

. . . . Nothing is wider of the mark than the mistaken accusation of materialism which has been levelled against us. Quite the contrary: from the point of view of our position, if one is to call the distinctive property of the individual representational life *spirituality*, one should say that social life is defined by its *hyperspirituality*. By this we mean that all the constituent attributes of mental life are found in it, but elevated to a very much higher power and in such a manner as to constitute something entirely new. Despite its metaphysical appearance, this word designates nothing more than a body of natural facts which are explained by natural causes. It does, however, warn us that the new world thus opened to science surpasses all others in complexity; it is not merely a lower field of study conceived in more ambitious terms, but one in which as yet unsuspected forces are at work, and of which the laws may not be discovered by the methods of interior analysis alone.

3

Social Facts and
Sociological Methodology

Durkheim is most intense about positivism in the Rules of Sociological Method, a book which some have claimed is a classic in the field of methodology and others have seen as merely a handbook of how to conduct social research as a Durkheimian. In his statement of methodology Durkheim is first concerned to establish the realm of the social as capable of scientific investigation. Social facts must be capable of being treated as objective things (comme les choses) and of being studied without subjective bias. The sociologist, being a social scientist, must put himself in the same state of mind as any other scientist, the physicist, the chemist, or the physiologist. The facts that can be treated as socially material things may be called "institutions." Sociology is the study of institutions, of ways of acting and thinking that are general to a collectivity of human beings. These institutions must be studied as manifestations of group life and not as mere conglomerations of individual behavior. Society is thus an institutional order of its own. The explanation of social facts requires the establishment of the functions of institutions in this order. This order has an internal constitution of its own; explanation must take place through it and not through states of individual consciousness.

Sociology is concerned with the stages through which the social order has moved in time. It must seek to discover the causes for changes from one stage to another stage and within each stage; that is, it seeks to explain and not merely to describe. It cannot accept the present stage of society as "the definitive state of humanity." Sociology is concerned with the characteristics of collective types and with the causes for change from type to type.

23

In arriving at causes for changes, sociology in Durkheim's view has one experimental method at its disposal, the method of concomitant variation. Statistical correlation, which is detailed analysis of concomitant variation between and among factors, is an indispensable aid to causal analysis. When Durkheim wrote the Rules, statistical techniques and knowledge were still relatively primitive, and much more was held out for them from the standpoint of causal analysis than has eventuated since. Statistical correlation betokens interdependence of factors, but causal relationship requires much more than proof of interdependence.

To explain a social fact it is necessary not only to treat it in its milieu in one instance of what Durkheim called a social species, but in its complete development in all social species, he tells us. The comparative method is not just part of sociology; it is imbedded in sociology—"It is sociology itself, in so far as it ceases to be purely descriptive and aspires to account for facts."

As a science sociology is tied to no philosophical system and to no political doctrine, according to Durkheim. In its method it is independent of both. Ties to a philosophy or political doctrine would deprive sociology of its objectivity and therefore of its scientific status. Yet Durkheim's own works serve as a reminder that devotion to objectivity and science is itself a philosophical doctrine and involves a political allegiance to freedom of investigation.

In the Rules Durkheim continues to stress that sociology is tied to no psychology of the individual but rather to collective psychology. But his view of the psychology of the individual is really quite old-fashioned; in fact, it is very shop-worn in its exclusive emphasis upon motor, sensory, and cerebral phenomena and in its time-bound inability to come to terms with the determination of "social" behavior by unconscious yet dynamic psychic processes in the individual.

What Durkheim's statement of methodology achieves is a systemization of the investigatory techniques he had used in the study of the division of labor and in the study of suicide, techniques he ties in with positivist doctrines relative to objectivity, externality, and causation. Durkheim did not have at his disposal the codified techniques of interviewing and opinion surveying we now have (although he propounded their basic logic in Suicide as Hanan C. Selvin* has shown), nor the vast storehouse of statistical data now available

* In an article in the *American Journal of Sociology* in 1958.

through governmental and private agencies. He himself was not a sociological "field" worker. Nor in his anthropological work did he ever go out and live among primitive peoples, but took his material from reports and books by others as in The Elementary Forms of the Religious Life. His positivism undoubtedly can be made to fit in with contemporary research techniques in sociology, but in the light of his vast learning he would certainly find intolerable some of the minutiae which pass for problems worthy of research today. Nor would his type of learned mind lend itself to a defense of contemporary research that puffs itself up on the techniques but shows little knowledge of subject-matter.

What Is a Social Fact? *

[The social realm] . . . is a category of facts with very distinctive characteristics: it consists of ways of acting, thinking, and feeling, external to the individual, and endowed with a power of coercion, by reason of which they control him. These ways of thinking could not be confused with biological phenomena, since they consist of representations and of actions; nor with psychological phenomena, which exist only in the individual consciousness and through it. They constitute, thus, a new variety of phenomena; and it is to them exclusively that the term "social" ought to be applied. And this term fits them quite well, for it is clear that, since their source is not in the individual, their substratum can be no other than society, either the political society as a whole or some one of the partial groups it includes, such as religious denominations, political, literary, and occupational associations, etc. On the other hand, this term "social" applies to them exclusively, for it has a distinct meaning only if it designates exclusively the phenomena which are not included in any of the categories of facts that have already been established and classified. These ways of thinking and acting therefore constitute the proper domain of sociology. It is true that, when we define them with this word "constraint," we risk shocking the zealous partisans of absolute individualism. For those who profess the complete autonomy of the individual,

---

* From The Rules of Sociological Method, pp. 3–4, 6–10, 13; from the preface to the second edition, pp. xliii, xlv, xlvii, lii, lv, lvi, lvii.

man's dignity is diminished whenever he is made to feel that he is not completely self-determinant. It is generally accepted today, however, that most of our ideas and our tendencies are not developed by ourselves but come to us from without. How can they become a part of us except by imposing themselves upon us? This is the whole meaning of our definition. And it is generally accepted, moreover, that social constraint is not necessarily incompatible with the individual personality.

. . . . .

. . . Sociological phenomena cannot be defined by their universality. A thought which we find in every individual consciousness, a movement repeated by all individuals, is not thereby a social fact. If sociologists have been satisfied with defining them by this characteristic, it is because they confused them with what one might call their reincarnation in the individual. It is, however, the collective aspects of the beliefs, tendencies, and practices of a group that characterize truly social phenomena. As for the forms that the collective states assume when refracted in the individual, these are things of another sort. This duality is clearly demonstrated by the fact that these two orders of phenomena are frequently found dissociated from one another. Indeed, certain of these social manners of acting and thinking acquire, by reason of their repetition, a certain rigidity which on its own account crystallizes them, so to speak, and isolates them from the particular events which reflect them. They thus acquire a body, a tangible form, and constitute a reality in their own right, quite distinct from the individual facts which produce it. Collective habits are inherent not only in the successive acts which they determine but, by a privilege of which we find no example in the biological realm, they are given permanent expression in a formula which is repeated from mouth to mouth, transmitted by education, and fixed even in writing. Such is the origin and nature of legal and moral rules, popular aphorisms and proverbs, articles of faith wherein religious or political groups condense their beliefs, standards of taste established by literary schools, etc. None of these can be found entirely reproduced in the applications made of them by individuals, since they can exist even without being actually applied. . . .

. . . . Currents of opinion, with an intensity varying according to the time and place, impel certain groups either to more marriages, for example, or to more suicides, or to a higher or lower birth-rate, etc. These currents are plainly social facts. At first sight they seem inseparable from the forms they take in individual cases. But statistics furnish us with the means of isolating them. They are, in fact, represented with considerable exactness by the rates of births, marriages, and suicides, that is, by the number obtained by dividing the average annual total of marriages, births, suicides, by the number of persons whose ages lie within the range in which marriages, births, and suicides occur. Since each of these figures contains all the individual cases indiscriminately, the individual circumstances which may have had a share in the production of the phenomenon are neutralized and, consequently, do not contribute to its determination. The average, then, expresses a certain state of the group mind (*l'âme collective*).

Such are social phenomena, when disentangled from all foreign matter. As for their individual manifestations, these are indeed, to a certain extent, social, since they partly reproduce a social model. Each of them also depends, and to a large extent, on the organo-psychological constitution of the individual and on the particular circumstances in which he is placed. Thus they are not sociological phenomena in the strict sense of the word. They belong to two realms at once; one could call them sociopsychological. They interest the sociologist without constituting the immediate subject matter of sociology. There exist in the interior of organisms similar phenomena, compound in their nature, which form in their turn the subject matter of the "hybrid sciences," such as physiological chemistry, for example.

.   .   .   .   .

We thus arrive at the point where we can formulate and delimit in a precise way the domain of sociology. It comprises only a limited group of phenomena. A social fact is to be recognized by the power of external coercion which it exercises or is capable of exercising over individuals, and the presence of this power may be recognized in its turn either by the existence of some specific sanction or by the resistance offered against every individual effort that tends to violate it. One can, however, define it also by its diffusion within the group, provided that, in conformity with our previous remarks, one takes care to add as a second and essential characteristic that its own existence is independent of the individual forms it assumes in its diffusion. This last criterion is perhaps, in certain cases, easier to apply than the preceding one. In fact, the constraint is easy to ascertain when it expresses itself externally by some direct reaction of society, as is the case in law, morals, beliefs, customs, and even fashions. But when it is only indirect, like the constraint which an economic organization

exercises, it cannot always be so easily detected. Generality combined
with externality may, then, be easier to establish. Moreover, this
second definition is but another form of the first; for if a mode of
behavior whose existence is external to individual consciousnesses
becomes general, this can only be brought about by its being imposed
upon them.

. . . . .

. . . . Our definition will then include the whole relevant range of
facts if we say: *A social fact is every way of acting, fixed or not, capable
of exercising on the individual an external constraint; or again, every
way of acting which is general throughout a given society, while at
the same time existing in its own right independent of its individual
manifestations.*

. . . . .

The proposition which states that social facts are to be treated as
things—the proposition at the very basis of our method—is one of
those which have provoked most contradiction. It has been considered
not only paradoxical but ridiculous for us to compare the realities of
the social world with those of the external world. But our critics have
curiously misinterpreted the meaning and import of this analogy, for
it was not our intention to reduce the higher to the lower forms of
being, but merely to claim for the higher forms a degree of reality
at least equal to that which is readily granted to the lower. We assert
not that social facts are material things but that they are things by
the same right as material things, although they differ from them in
type.

. . . Things include all objects of knowledge that cannot be conceived by purely mental activity, those that require for their conception data from outside the mind, from observations and experiments,
those which are built up from the more external and immediately
accessible characteristics to the less visible and more profound. To
treat the facts of a certain order as things is not, then, to place them
in a certain category of reality but to assume a certain mental attitude
toward them on the principle that when approaching their study we
are absolutely ignorant of their nature, and that their characteristic
properties, like the unknown causes on which they depend, cannot
be discovered by even the most careful introspection.

. . . . .

Our principle, then, implies no metaphysical conception, no specu-
lation about the fundamental nature of beings. What it demands is

that the sociologist put himself in the same state of mind as the physicist, chemist, or physiologist when he probes into a still unexplored region of the scientific domain. When he penetrates the social world, he must be aware that he is penetrating the unknown; he must feel himself in the presence of facts whose laws are as unsuspected as were those of life before the era of biology; he must be prepared for discoveries which will surprise and disturb him. . . .

. . . . .

Another proposition has been argued no less vehemently than the preceding one, namely, that social phenomena are external to individuals. Today our critics grant, willingly enough, that the facts of individual and of collective life are not altogether coterminous; one can even say that a quite general, if not unanimous, understanding on this point is in process of being achieved. Practically all sociologists now demand a separate existence for their science; but because society is composed only of individuals, the common-sense view still holds that sociology is a superstructure built upon the substratum of the individual consciousness and that otherwise it would be suspended in a social vacuum.

. . . . .

In no case can sociology simply borrow from psychology any one of its principles in order to apply it, as such, to social facts. Collective thought, in its form as in its matter, must be studied in its entirety, in and for itself, with an understanding of its peculiar nature. How much it resembles the thought of individuals must be left for future investigation. It is a problem which is rather within the jurisdiction of general philosophy and abstract logic than in the science of social facts.

. . . We gave a definition of social facts as ways of acting or thinking with the peculiar characteristic of exercising a coercive influence on individual consciousnesses. Confusion has arisen on this score which requires comment.

. . . . .

. . . . The peculiar characteristic of social constraint is that it is due, not to the rigidity of certain molecular arrangements, but to the prestige with which certain representations are invested. It is true that habits, either physical or social, have in certain respects this same feature. They dominate us and impose beliefs and practices upon us. But they rule us from within, for they are in every case an integral part of ourself. On the contrary, social beliefs and practices act on us from without; thus the influence exerted by them differs fundamentally from the effect of habit.

. . . . These ways of thinking and acting exist in their own right. The individual finds them completely formed, and he cannot evade or change them. He is therefore obliged to reckon with them. It is difficult (we do not say impossible) for him to modify them in direct proportion to the extent that they share in the material and moral supremacy of society over its members. Of course, the individual plays a role in their genesis. But in order that there may be a social fact, several individuals, at the very least, must have contributed their action; and in this joint activity is the origin of a new fact. Since this joint activity takes place outside each one of us (for a plurality of consciousnesses enters into it), its necessary effect is to fix, to institute outside us, certain ways of acting and certain judgments which do not depend on each particular will taken separately. It has been pointed out that the word "institution" well expresses this special mode of reality, provided that the ordinary significance of it be slightly extended. One can, indeed, without distorting the meaning of this expression, designate as "institutions" all the beliefs and all the modes of conduct instituted by the collectivity. Sociology can then be defined as the science of institutions, of their genesis and of their functioning.[1]

---

[1] Because beliefs and social practices thus come to us from without, it does not follow that we receive them passively or without modification. In reflecting on collective institutions and assimilating them for ourselves, we individualize them and impart to them more or less personal characteristics. Similary, in reflecting on the physical world, each of us colors it after his own fashion, and different individuals adapt themselves differently to the same physical environment. It is for this reason that each one of us creates, in a measure, his own morality, religion, and mode of life. There is no conformity to social convention that does not comprise an entire range of individual shades. It is nonetheless true that this field of variations is a limited one. It verges on nonexistence or is very restricted in that circle of religious and moral affairs where deviation easily becomes crime. It is wider in all that concerns economic life. But, sooner or later, even in the latter instance, one encounters the limit that cannot be crossed.

Observation of Social Facts *

The first and most fundamental rule is: *Consider social facts as things.*

The first corollary is: *All preconceptions must be eradicated.* . . .

. . . . Our second corollary: *The subject matter of every sociological study should comprise a group of phenomena defined in advance by certain common external characteristics, and all phenomena so defined should be included within this group.*

When . . . the sociologist undertakes the investigation of some order of social facts, he must endeavor to consider them from an aspect that is independent of their individual manifestations. . . .

Explanation of Social Facts †

When . . . the explanation of a social phenomenon is undertaken, we must seek separately the efficient cause which produces it and the function it fulfils. We use the word "function," in preference to "end" or "purpose," precisely because social phenomena do not generally exist for the useful results they produce. We must determine whether there is a correspondence between the fact under consideration and the general needs of the social organism, and in what this correspondence consists, without occupying ourselves with whether it has been intentional or not. All these questions of intention are too subjective to allow of scientific treatment.

. . . . The determination of function is . . . necessary for the complete explanation of the phenomena. Indeed, if the usefulness of a fact is not the cause of its existence, it is generally necessary that it be useful in order that it may maintain itself. For the fact that it

* From *The Rules of Sociological Method*, pp. 14, 31, 35, 45.
† From *The Rules of Sociological Method*, pp. 95, 97, 110–11, 112–13.

is not useful suffices to make it harmful, since in that case it costs effort without bringing in any returns. If, then, the majority of social phenomena had this parasitic character, the budget of the organism would have a deficit and social life would be impossible. Consequently, to have a satisfactory understanding of the latter, it is necessary to show how the phenomena comprising it combine in such a way as to put society in harmony with itself and with the environment external to it. No doubt, the current formula, which defines social life as a correspondence between the internal and the external milieu, is only an approximation; however, it is in general true. Consequently, to explain a social fact it is not enough to show the cause on which it depends; we must also, at least in most cases, show its function in the establishment of social order.

We arrive . . . at the following principle: *The determining cause of a social fact should be sought among the social facts preceding it and not among the states of the individual consciousness*. . . . The function of a social fact cannot but be social, i.e., it consists of the production of socially useful effects. To be sure, it may and does happen that it also serves the individual. But this happy result is not its immediate cause. We can then complete the preceding proposition by saying: *The function of a social fact ought always to be sought in its relation to some social end*.

. . . If the determining condition of social phenomena is, as we have shown, the very fact of association, the phenomena ought to vary with the forms of that association, i.e., according to the ways in which the constituent parts of society are grouped. Since, moreover, a given aggregate, formed by the union of elements of all kinds which enter into the composition of a society, constitutes its internal environment (just as the aggregate of anatomic elements, together with the way in which they are disposed in space, constitutes the internal milieu of organisms), we can say: *The first origins of all social processes of any importance should be sought in the internal constitution of the social group*.

It is possible to be even more precise. The elements which make up this milieu are of two kinds: things and persons. Besides material objects incorporated into the society, there must also be included the products of previous social activity: law, established customs, literary and artistic works, etc. But it is clear that the impulsion which determines social transformations can come from neither the material nor the immaterial, for neither possesses a motivating power. There is, assuredly, occasion to take them into consideration in the explanations one attempts. They bear with a certain weight on social evolution, whose speed and even direction vary according to the nature of these elements; but they contain nothing of what is required to put it in motion. They are the matter upon which the social forces of society act, but by themselves they release no social energy. As an active factor, then, the human milieu itself remains.

The principal task of the sociologist ought to be, therefore, to discover the different aspects of this milieu which can exert some influence on the course of social phenomena.

Sociological Explanation
vs. Historical Explanation*

But the significance attributed by us to the social and, more particularly, the human milieu does not imply that we must see in it a sort of ultimate and absolute fact beyond which there is no reason for inquiry. It is evident, on the contrary, that its condition at each moment of history is itself a result of social causes, some of which are inherent in the society itself, while others depend on interaction between this society and its neighbors. Moreover, science is not concerned with first-causes, in the absolute sense of the word. For science, a fact is primary simply when it is general enough to explain a great number of other facts. Now, the social milieu is certainly a factor of this kind, since the changes which are produced in it, whatever may be their causes, have their repercussions in all directions in the social organism and cannot fail to affect to some extent each of its functions.

. . . . .

This conception of the social milieu, as the determining factor of collective evolution, is of the highest importance. For, if we reject it, sociology cannot establish any relations of causality. In fact, if we eliminate this type of cause, there are no concomitant conditions on which social phenomena can depend; for if the external social milieu, i.e., that which is formed by the surrounding societies, can take some

* From *The Rules of Sociological Method*, pp. 115–16, 117, 118, 119–21.

action, it is only that of attack and defense; and, further, it can make its influence felt only by the intermediary of the internal social milieu. The principal causes of historical development would not be found, then, among the concomitant circumstances; they would all be in the past. They would themselves form a part of this development, of which they would constitute simply older phases. The present events of social life would originate not in the present state of society but in prior events, from historical precedents; and sociological explanations would consist exclusively in connecting the present with the past.

.   .   .   .   .

All that we can observe experimentally in the species is a series of changes among which a causal bond does not exist. The antecedent state does not produce the subsequent one, but the relation between them is exclusively chronological. Under these circumstances, all scientific prevision is impossible. We can, indeed, say that certain conditions have succeeded one another up to the present, but not in what order they will henceforth succeed one another, since the cause on which they are supposed to depend is not scientifically determined or determinable. Ordinarily, it is true, we admit that evolution will take the same direction as in the past; but this is a mere postulate. Nothing assures us that the overt phenomena express so completely the nature of this tendency that we may be able to foretell the objective to which this tendency aspires as distinct from those through which it has successively passed. Why, indeed, should the direction it follows be rectilinear?

.   .   .   .   .

From another angle, it is again with relation to this same milieu that the utility or, as we have called it, the function of social phenomena must be measured. Among the changes caused by the social milieu, only those serve a purpose which are compatible with the current state of society, since the milieu is the essential condition of collective existence. From this point of view again, the conception we have just expounded is, we believe, fundamental; for it alone enables us to explain how the useful character of social phenomena can vary, without however depending on a volitional social order. If we represent historic evolution as impelled by a sort of vital urge which pushes men forward, since a propelling tendency can have but one goal, there can be only one point of reference with relation to which the usefulness or harmfulness of social phenomena is calculated. Consequently, there can, and does, exist only one type of social organization that fits humanity perfectly; and the different historical societies are only successive approximations to this single model. It is unnecessary to show that, today, such a simple view is irreconcilable with the recognized variety and complexity of social forms. If, on the contrary, the fitness or unfitness of institutions can only be established in connection with a given milieu, since these milieus are diverse, there is a diversity of points of reference and hence of types which, while being qualitatively distinct from one another, are all equally grounded in the nature of the social milieus.

The question just treated is, then, closely connected with that of the constitution of social types. If there are social species, it is because collective life depends, above all, on concomitant conditions which present a certain diversity. If, on the contrary, all the principal causes of social events were in the past, each society would no longer be anything but the prolongation of its predecessor, and the different societies would lose their individuality and would become only diverse moments of one and the same evolution. Since, on the other hand, the constitution of the social milieu results from the mode of composition of the social aggregates—and these two expressions are essentially synonymous—we now have the proof that there are no more essential characteristics than those assigned by us as the basis of sociological classifications. Finally, we must now understand, better than previously, how unjust it would be for our critics to point to these words, "external conditions" and "milieu," as an accusation that our method seeks the sources of life outside the living being. On the contrary, the considerations just stated lead us back to the idea that the causes of social phenomena are internal to society. Rather, we ourselves could more justly criticize the theory which derives society from the individual for trying to extract the internal from the external (since it explains the social being by something other than itself) and the greater from the smaller (since it undertakes to deduce the whole from the part). . . .

Concomitant Variation and
Experimental Method in Sociology *

. . . [For] the method of concomitant variations or correlation
. . . to be reliable, it is not necessary that all the variables differing
from those which we are comparing shall have been strictly excluded.
The mere parallelism of the series of values presented by the two
phenomena, provided that it has been established in a sufficient
number and variety of cases, is proof that a relationship exists between
them. Its validity is due to the fact that the concomitant variations
display the causal relationship not by coincidence, as the preceding
ones do, but intrisically. It does not simply show us two facts which
accompany or exclude one another externally, so that there is no
direct proof that they are united by an internal bond; on the contrary,
it shows them as mutually influencing each other in a continuous
manner, at least so far as their quality is concerned. This interaction,
it itself, suffices to demonstrate that they are not foreign to each
other.

The manner in which a phenomenon develops expresses its nature.
For two developments to correspond to each other, there must also
be a correspondence in the natures manifested by them. Constant
concomitance is, then, a law in itself, whatever may be the condition
of the phenomena excluded from the comparison. . . . When two
phenomena vary directly with each other, this relationship must be
accepted even when, in certain cases, one of these phenomena should
be present without the other. For it may be either that the cause has
been prevented from producing its effect by the action of some contrary cause or that it is present but in a form different from the one
previously observed. No doubt, we need, as we say, to examine the
facts anew; but certainly we must not abandon hastily the results of
a methodically conducted demonstration.

It is true that the laws established by this procedure are not always
presented at the outset in the form of relations of causality. The
concomitance may be due not to the fact that one phenomenon is
the cause of the other but to the fact that they are both the effects

* From *The Rules of Sociological Method*, pp. 130–31, 132, 133–34, 135–36.

of the same cause, or, again, that there exists between them a third phenomenon, interposed but unperceived, which is the effect of the first and the cause of the second. The results to which this method leads need, therefore, to be interpreted. But what experimental method is there which obtains mechanically a relation of causality without some analysis of the observed data?

. . . . .

But there is another reason which makes the method of concomitant variations the instrument par excellence of sociological research. . . . The conclusions of sociologists have often been discredited because they have . . . occupied themselves more with accumulating documents than with selecting and criticizing them. Thus it often happens that they assign the same value to the confused, hastily made observations of travelers as to the carefully prepared texts of history. When we see these demonstrations, not only can we not avoid saying to ourselves that a single fact could invalidate them but the very facts on which they are established do not always inspire confidence.

The method of concomitant variations compels us to accept neither these incomplete enumerations nor these superficial observations. In order to obtain results, a few facts suffice. As soon as one has proved that, in a certain number of cases, two phenomena vary with one another, one is certain of being in the presence of a law. Having no need to be numerous, the documents can be selected and, further, studied more closely by the sociologist. He will then be able to take as the principal material for his inductions the societies whose beliefs, traditions, customs, and law have taken shape in written and authentic documents. To be sure, he will not spurn the information offered by uncritical ethnography (there are no facts which may be disdained by the scientist), but he will put them in their true place. Instead of making this the center of gravity of his researches, he will in general utilize it only as a supplement to historical data; or, at the very least, he will try to confirm it by the latter. Not only will he thus limit more intelligently the extent of his comparisons, but he will conduct them with a more critical spirit; for, by the very fact that he will confine himself to a restricted order of facts, he will be able to check them with more care. No doubt, he does not need again to work over the research of historians, but neither can he welcome passively and naïvely every bit of information which comes to his hand.

. . . . .

Unless it is applied with care and precision, however, it does not produce its best results. One proves nothing when, as so often happens, one is content to show by more or less numerous examples that, in scattered cases, the facts have varied as the hypothesis demands. From these sporadic and fragmentary agreements one can draw no general conclusion. To illustrate the idea is not to demonstrate it. It is necessary to compare not isolated variations but a series of systematically arranged variations of wide range, in which the individual items tie up with one another in as continuous a gradation as possible. For the variations of a phenomenon permit inductive generalizations only if they reveal clearly the manner in which they develop under given circumstances. There must be between them the same sequence as between the different stages of a given natural evolution; and, in addition, the evolutionary trend that they establish ought to be sufficiently extended as to lend some certainty to its direction.

Explanation and Comparative Sociology*

. . . To explain a social institution belonging to a given species, one will compare its different forms, not only among peoples of that species but in all preceding species as well. For example, in the matter of domestic organization the most rudimentary type that has ever existed will first be established, in order that the manner in which it grew progressively more complex may then be followed, step by step. This method, which may be called "genetic," would give at once the analysis and the synthesis of the phenomenon. For, on the one hand, it would show us the separate elements composing it, by the very fact that it would allow us to see the process of accretion or action. At the same time, thanks to this wide field of comparison, we should be in a much better position to determine the conditions on which depend their formation. Consequently, one cannot explain a social fact of any complexity except by following its complete development through all social species. Comparative sociology is not a particular branch of sociology; it is sociology itself, in so far as it ceases to be purely descriptive and aspires to account for facts.

In the course of these extended comparisons, an error is often committed with correspondingly misleading results. At times, in order to judge the direction in which social events develop, it has happened

* From *The Rules of Sociological Method*, pp. 138–40.

that scholars have simply compared what occurs at the decline of each species with what happens at the beginning of the succeeding species. Proceeding thus, it has been said, for example, that the weakening of religious beliefs and all traditionalism could never be anything but a transitory phenomenon in the life of peoples, because it appears only during the last period of their existence and ceases as soon as a new stage begins. But, with such a method, one is tempted to take as the regular and necessary march of progress that which was simply the effect of an entirely different cause. In fact, any certain stage of a young society is not simply the prolongation of the stage of the preceding declining society. On the contrary, it is conditioned in part by the very fact of its youth, which prevents the products of the knowledge asquired by former peoples from being immediately assimilated and utilized. Thus the child receives from his parents faculties and predispositions which come into play in his life only belatedly. It is therefore possible that the return to traditionalism observed at the beginning of the history of each individual society is due not to the fact that an eclipse of the phenomenon can be only transitory but to the special conditions in which every young society is placed. The comparison can be valid only if we remove this disturbing factor of age. To arrive at a just comparison, *it will suffice to consider the societies compared at the same period of their development.* Thus, in order to know in what direction a social phenomenon is evolving, one will compare the youth of each species with the youth of the succeeding species, and, according as (from one of these stages to the next) it presents more, less, or equal complexity, one can say that it progresses, retrogresses, or maintains itself.

Methodology and the Progress of Sociology[*]

To sum up, the distinctive characteristics of our method are as follows: First, it is entirely independent of philosophy. . . .

With reference to practical social doctrines, our method permits and commands the same independence. Sociology thus understood will be neither individualistic, communistic, nor socialistic in the sense commonly given these words. . . .

[*] From *The Rules of Sociological Method*, pp. 141, 142, 143, 144, 145.

In the second place, our method is objective. It is dominated entirely by the idea that social facts are things and must be treated as such. . . .

If we consider social facts as things, we consider them as *social things*. The third trait that characterizes our method is that it is exclusively sociological. . . .

Sociology is . . . not an auxiliary of any other science; it is itself a distinct and autonomous science, and the feeling of the specificity of social reality is indeed so necessary to the sociologist that only distinctly sociological training can prepare him to grasp social facts intelligently.

4

Social Evolution

Durkheim was early swept into the currents of evolutionary thinking that had been instigated in the social sciences by developments in biology. A search for laws of social development and for the stages through which western society had passed on its way through the nineteenth century was being vigorously pursued on both sides of the Atlantic. Even before Darwin, however, Auguste Comte had raised the problem of the stages of social development. In his doctoral dissertation on the division of labor in society, Durkheim devoted himself to this general field of investigation. He sought to prove that the development of the division of labor in society with its accompanying differentiation of occupations and multiplication of relatively autonomous groups was the key to discovering laws of general social development.

In 1893, when Durkheim's work on the division of labor appeared, the concept of "solidarity," referring to the cohesion of human groups into a social unity, was being bandied about in France. Durkheim wove this skein of thought into evolutionary doctrine, finding different types of solidarity at different stages of social evolution. Modern society, he held, had evolved from the stage of mechanical solidarity into the stage of organic solidarity, from the stage of collective standardization of behavior to that of individual differences. Modern society manifests not the simple unity of a primitive organism but a unity achieved through the interdependence of differentiated parts as in higher organisms. As a leading index of how this development took place Durkheim used law. He found criminal law with repressive sanctions supreme in lower or primitive societies, but in higher or modern societies he found a steady decline in the scope of criminal sanctions and a growth of civil or restitutive sanctions.

What is called "civilization" involved for Durkheim the growth of individual rights through the division of labor and the proliferation of autonomous groups with independence of action in specialized areas of social life. These processes may not always work out a smooth solidarity; then anomy appears—the absence of moral rules appropriate to the state of individual relationships that have come into existence.

The state of the division of labor in a society affords the basis for explaining the existence of the kinds and types of social organization present there. In the Rules Durkheim points out that societies can be classified according to the degree of organization they present, taking as the basis of comparison the perfectly simple society or the society of one segment. Within each type thus classified, Durkheim says we can distinguish different varieties according to whether a complete coalescence of the initial segments does or does not appear. Unfortunately, Durkheim never did spell out in detail the varieties of organic solidarity through analysis of the various stages of development of western society. Had he done so, he might even have concluded that just two categories of solidarity—mechanical and organic —are insufficient to encompass the whole course of social evolution.

In developing his theory of social evolution through advances in the division of labor, Durkheim wandered far and wide—from prescriptions for the establishment of a science of morals, to the concepts of collective conscience and collective representations, to anomy, to primitive society, to the sociology of religion, and to law and sanction, among other areas. The topics had to be treated with broad brush strokes. But even so, the intellectual stimulation and majestic learning that Durkheim's work on the division of labor offers were in 1893 and are still today outstanding examples of the talents an enlightened sociology demands of its trained proponents.

Mechanical and Organic Solidarity*

. . . We shall recognize . . . two kinds of positive solidarity which bear the following characters:

1. The first binds the individual to society without mediation. In

---

* From *Division of Labor in Society*, pp. 129-31. The several selections from this source have been retranslated for this volume by George Simpson and Louis Lister.

the second, he is dependent upon the parts of which society is composed.

2. Society is seen in a different aspect in each case. In the first, what we call society is a more or less organized totality of beliefs and sentiments common to all the members of the group: this is the collective type. In the second case, on the contrary, social solidarity involves definite relations bound together in a system of different specialized functions. These two types of society really are two aspects of one and the same reality. But they must nevertheless be separated.

3. This second difference gives rise to another which is going to help us characterize and name the two kinds of solidarity.

The first is strong only in so far as the ideas and tendencies common to all the members of the society are greater in number and intensity than those which pertain to each member personally. This type of solidarity increases with the extent of the preponderance of the common ideas and tendencies over the personal ones. Now, what distinguishes a personality from the rest of the group is the possession of qualities which are individual and separate. So this type of solidarity increases in inverse ratio to personality. There are in each of us, as we have said, two consciences: one which is common to our group in its entirety and which, consequently, is not ourself but the society living and acting within us; the other, on the contrary, represents that in us which is personal and distinct, that which makes us an individual.[1] The solidarity which is based on likeness is at its maximum when the collective conscience completely envelops our whole conscience and coincides in all points with it. But then individuality is nil. Individuality arises only if the community recedes. There are in human consciousness two contrary forces, one centripetal, the other centrifugal, which cannot both increase simultaneously. We cannot at one and the same time develop ourselves in two opposite senses. If we have a lively desire to think and act for ourselves, we cannot be strongly inclined to think and act as others do. If our ideal is to present a singular and personal appearance, we do not want to resemble everybody else. Our personality fades, so to speak, under the influence of solidarity based on likeness because we are no longer ourselves but the collective being.

The social molecules which cohere only in this manner can move together, as in the case with inorganic molecules, only to the extent that they cannot move individually. That is why we propose to call

[1] These two consciences are not distinct regions but interpenetrate from all sides.

this type of solidarity mechanical. The term does not signify that it is produced by mechanical and artificial means. We call it that only by analogy to the cohesion through which the elements of inanimate bodies are united as opposed to the cohesion through which living organisms are united. What justifies this term is that the link which thus unites the individual to the society is wholly analogous to that which links a person and his possession. In this light, the individual conscience is simply a reflection of the collective type and follows all of its movements as the possessed object follows those of its owner. In societies where this type of solidarity is highly developed, the individual does not belong to himself. . . . Society can literally do with him as it wishes. Thus in these social types personal rights are not yet distinguished from property rights.

It is quite otherwise with the solidarity which is produced by the division of labor. Whereas the previous type implies that individuals resemble each other, this type presumes their difference. The first type is possible only in so far as the individual personality is absorbed into the collective personality; the second is possible only if each one has an individual sphere of action, consequently a personality. The collective conscience must therefore allow a part of the individual conscience to appear if special functions are to be established, functions which the collective conscience cannot itself carry out. The more this area is extended, the stronger is the cohesion which results from this solidarity. The greater the division of labor, the greater the dependence of the individual on society, on the one hand; on the other hand, the more specialized the individual, the more personal his activity. Yet no matter how specialized the activity it is never completely original. Even in the exercise of a profession we conform to usages, to practices which are common to the whole profession. But even in this case the yoke that we submit to is much less heavy than when society completely controls us, and it leaves much more place open for the free play of our initiative. Here then, the individuality of all grows at the same time as that of its parts. Society becomes more capable of collective movement at the same time that each of its elements has more individual movement. This solidarity resembles that which we observe among the higher animals. Each organ, in effect, has its special physiognomy, its autonomy. Yet the unity of the organism increases the more marked the individuality of its parts is. By virtue of this analogy we propose to call the solidarity which is due to the division of labor, organic.

Evolution from Mechanical to Organic Solidarity Relative to Crime, Religion, and Proverbs *

Mechanical solidarity generally is not only a weaker link than organic solidarity but it also decreases in importance as social evolution advances.

. . . . .

. . . Strong and defined states of the common conscience are the roots of penal law. . . . These states are fewer in number today and . . . their number progressively diminishes as societies approach our present type. The average intensity and the average degree of definiteness of collective states have . . . diminished. We cannot conclude from this fact that the total extent of the common conscience has narrowed for it may be that the region to which penal law corresponds has contracted and that the remainder have expanded. The common conscience can have fewer strong and defined states but a much greater number of other states. But this growth, if actual, is altogether equivalent to that which is produced in the individual conscience for the latter has grown at least to the same degree. Though there are more things common to all, there are also many more that are personal to each. There is, indeed, every reason for believing that the personal ones have increased more than the others since the differences between men have become more pronouncd as they have become more cultivated. . . . It is . . . at least probable that in each individual conscience the personal sphere is much greater than the collective. Certainly the relation between them has at least remained the same. In this last case mechanical solidarity has gained nothing even if it has not lost anything. If, on the other hand, we discover that the collective conscience has become weaker and more indefinite, we can rest assured that there has been an enfeeblement of mechanical solidarity. . . .

It would serve no purpose in behalf of proof of this enfeeblement to compare the number of rules with repressive sanctions in different

* From *Division of Labor in Society*, pp. 152–54, 168–73.

social types since the number of rules does not vary exactly with the sentiments the rules represent. The same sentiment can actually be offended in several different ways and thus give rise to several rules without diversifying itself in so doing. Because there are now more ways of acquiring property, there are also more ways of stealing, but the *sentiment* of respect for the property of another has not on that account increased. Because individual personality has developed and encompasses more areas, there are more criminal attacks possible against it but the sentiment that they offend is always the same. It is necessary for us, then, not to count rules but to group them in classes and sub-classes according as they relate to the same sentiment or to different sentiments or to different varieties of the same sentiment. We shall thus establish criminological types and their basic varieties; their number is necessarily equal to that of strong and definite states of the common conscience. The more numerous the latter are, the more criminal types there ought to be; consequently, the variations in one should be exactly reflected in the variations of the other. . . . It is quite evident that such a classification will be neither complete nor perfectly rigorous. It is, however, sufficiently exact for our purposes. It certainly encompasses all the present criminological types; it may omit only some which have disappeared. But as we wish to demonstrate precisely the fact that their number has diminished, these omissions would only strengthen our conclusion.

.　.　.　.　.

It has often been said that religion has throughout history consisted of the totality of every sort of belief and sentiment pertaining to the relations of man with a being or beings whom he regards as superior to himself. But such a definition is clearly inadequate. Surely there are many rules of conduct and of belief which are clearly religious but which are applicable to a totally different kind of relationship. Religion forbids the Jew to eat certain meats and orders him to dress in a set way. It requires holding an established opinion on the nature of man and of the external world and on the origin of the world. Religion wields general sway over legal, moral, and economic relationships. Its sphere of activity extends well beyond the interaction of man with the divine order. Moreover, we know that there is at least one religion without a divinity (Buddhism). Once this fact had been established it should have been clear that religion was not to be defined through the idea of God. Finally, if the extraordinary authority th-* *he believer vests in the divinity can account for the special prestige of everything religious, it remains to be explained how men have been led to attribute such an authority to a being who in the opinion of the world is in many cases, if not always, a product of their imaginations. Nothing comes from nothing; this power must have come to God from somewhere. Consequently, this formulation of what religion is does not get to the heart of the matter.

With the abandonment of the divine as the essential element of religion, the characteristic clearly inhering in all religious ideas and sentiments is that they are held in common by a group of individuals having a common life and that they possess a strong average intensity. That a rather strong opinion held by men in the same community inevitably takes on a religious character is assuredly a regular occurrence. This opinion arouses in men's minds the same respect and feeling of reverence as religious beliefs properly speaking. Hence it is altogether probable (although this short discussion undoubtedly cannot be taken as a rigorous proof) that religion, too, occupies a region at the very center of the common conscience. This region, to be sure, must be clearly delineated and distinguished from the region occupied by penal law; it is, indeed, often confused with the latter in whole or in part. Such problems require study but their solution does not bear directly on the highly probable hypothesis we just propounded.

Now, one truth categorically established by history is that religion comes to embrace an ever smaller part of social life. Originally religion blankets everything; what is social then is religious; the two words are then synonymous. By a slow process political, economic, and scientific activities are freed from religious domination; they take place separately and assume a more accentuated temporal character.

God (if we are permitted such utterance) at first resident in all human relations, progressively leaves them. He abandons the world to men and their quarrels. Or if he continues to rule the world, it is from on high and at a distance. His sphere of action becomes more vague and indeterminate; more and more room is left free for human powers. The individual is then more self-contained, actually less acted upon; he emerges as a spontaneous actor. In short, not only does religion's domain not grow together or equally with the domain of temporal life but rather does it contract as time goes on. This retreat does not begin at any certain point in history but its stages can be followed throughout the course of social evolution. This retreat is therefore tied in with the conditions basic to the development of societies. It accordingly testifies to the fact that an ever smaller number of collective beliefs and sentiments persist which are collective and strong enough to partake of a religious character. Hence the average intensity of the common conscience progressively becomes weaker.

The exposition relative to religion extends the earlier one relative to penal law. It makes it possible to prove that the same law of retreat that holds for the emotional side of the common conscience holds also for its representational (or mental) side. Through the avenue of penal law we can reach only phenomena of feeling but through religion we can also reach ideas and theories.

Decrease in the number of proverbs, adages, and folk-sayings in the course of social development constitutes another proof that even collective representations grow progressively more indefinite.

Among primitive peoples statements of this kind are certainly very numerous. Most of the races of west Africa, Ellis tells us, have a large assortment of proverbs; there is at least one for each area of life. This is a characteristic they have in common with most peoples who have made little advance in civilization. More advanced societies were rich in proverbs only during the early years of existence. Later on they not only do not come forth with new proverbs but rather do they slowly drop off the old ones. Finally even these old ones end up in complete desuetude. Proof that lower societies are preeminently their chosen domain is afforded by the fact that today they are found current only in the least educated classes. Now, a proverb is a concise expression of a collective idea or sentiment relative to a definite group of things. There can assuredly not be beliefs or sentiments of this kind that are not expressed in this manner. Since every thought common to a large number of individuals tends to be expressed in an appropriate way, it is finally interned in a form which is also common among them. Every durable function elaborates an organ in its own image. Therefore it is incorrect to explain the decline of proverbs by referring to our taste for realism and our feeling for science. We do not posit so much careful precision or such disdain for metaphor on the language of conversation. Rather we tend to relish the old proverbs left to us. Moreover, metaphor is not an indispensable part of a proverb; it is one way, but not the only one, in which collective thought is distilled. Condensed statements finally become too confining for the variety of individual sentiments. Their unity is out of line with the differences which appear. Hence they can survive only by taking on a more general meaning and then slowly disappearing. The organ atrophies because its function is no longer exercised, that is, because there are fewer collective representations sufficiently definite to be encompassed in a tight mould.

Thus everything goes to prove that the evolution of the common conscience occurs in the way we have indicated. Clearly it does not grow as do individual consciences; in any case, as a whole it becomes weaker and vaguer. The collective type loses its strength and its forms become more indistinct and less clear. Of course, if this decline (as is often claimed) was an offshoot only of the very recent type of civilization we have known and an occurrence quite exceptional in the history of societies, we might well ask whether it will endure. In reality, however, this decline has been taking place uninterruptedly since earliest times. That is what we have meant to prove. Individualism and free thought do not date only from our times or from 1789 or from the Reformation or from scholasticism or from the collapse of Greek and Roman polytheism or from oriental theocracy. Individualism and free thought are not phenomena which begin at a set time but rather do they develop unceasingly throughout the course of history. To be sure this development is not rectilinear. The new societies which succeed antiquated social types never begin their careers at the precise place where their predecessors left off. How could they? What a child perpetuates is not the old or middle age of his parents but their own childhood. To account for the path that has been trod we must compare societies with their successors at the same period of their lives. We must compare Christian societies of the Middle Ages with primitive Rome, primitive Rome with the early Greek city-state, etc. We then see that this progress (or stated differently, this decline) occurs without a break in continuity. Here we come upon an inexorable law that it would be silly to challenge.

But that does not mean that the common conscience is threatened with total extinction. Rather it comes to consist of more and more very general and very indefinite ways of thinking and feeling which make possible a growing multitude of individual differences. There is one area, indeed, where it is strong and clear—the area relating to the individual. To the extent that all other beliefs and practices assume an increasingly smaller religious character, the individual becomes the object of a kind of religion. In behalf of personal dignity we have established a cult which like all vigorous cults already has its own superstitions. Hence it can indeed be called, if one wishes, a common faith. But such a faith is possible, first of all, only by the collapse of other faiths. Consequently it cannot achieve the same results as the multitude of ancient beliefs. There is no compensation for the loss. Furthermore, though common in that the community of men participate in it, this faith has the individual as its object. Though it impels all wills towards the same goal, this goal is not social. It accordingly occupies a completely exceptional place in the collective conscience. Though deriving all its power from society, yet it is not to society that it binds us; this faith binds us only to ourselves. Consequently it does not constitute a true social link. Here lies the reason for the just reproach against the speculative thinkers who have made this sentiment the sole foundation of their moral doctrine, the reproach that they undermine society. Hence we can reach the conclusion that all social links derivative from likeness progressively grow slack.

In and of itself this law is already enough to show the grandeur of the role of the division of labor. Since mechanical solidarity grows weaker, then either social life itself declines or another solidarity slowly takes the place of the one on the way out. A choice must be made. Vainly it might be contended that the collective conscience widens and grows stronger simultaneously with individual consciences. We have already clearly shown that the two terms have meanings inverse to each other. Yet social progress does not involve a steady disappearance of the collective conscience. Completely to the contrary, for the more advance made the deeper the feeling that societies have of themselves and their unity. There must then assuredly be some other social link productive of this result. This link can be none other than the one arising from the division of labor.

If, moreover, we remember that even where mechanical solidarity is strongest, it does not link men with the same power as the division of labor and that in addition it leaves outside its sphere of action the major part of present social phenomena, it becomes still clearer that social solidarity tends to become exclusively organic. It is the division of labor which more and more occupies the place formerly filled by the common conscience. It is mainly the division of labor which binds together the social groups of higher societies.

This function of the division of labor is a good deal more significant than the one ordinarily assigned to it by economists.

Civilization and the Division of Labor*

Through establishing the chief cause [change in the volume and in the density of societies] of the progress of the division of labor we have also established the essential element in what is called civilization.

Civilization too is an inexorable result of the changes occurring in the volume and in the density of societies. The development of science, art, and economic activity derives from human necessity. Men cannot exist without them under the new conditions into which they are thrust. When the number of individuals involved in social relations grows larger, they can survive only by increased specialization, by increased labor, by great refinement of their capacities. From this wholesale excitation there must come a higher degree of culture. Looked at in this way, civilization emerges not as a goal urging peoples on by its attractiveness to them, not as a thing of value foreseen and longed for, of which they seek to appropriate as much as possible by every means possible, but civilization emerges as the effect of a cause, as the inevitable result of a fixed situation. It is not the lodestar leading on historical development, the end which men seek to get closer to in order to be happier or morally better. Neither happiness nor morality necessarily increases with life's intensity. Men proceed because they have to; the speed of their procession depends upon the greater or lesser strength of the pressure they exert on one another, strength itself dependent upon their numbers.

But the above must not be taken to mean that civilization serves no purpose but rather that the services it renders are not the cause of its progress. It develops because it cannot fail to develop. Once on its way this development is found to be generally useful or at least utilizable. It fulfills needs aroused simultaneously with it since these needs depend upon the same causes. But this adjustment to needs occurs after the fact. Moreover, we must not overlook the fact that the benefits thus rendered by civilization are not clear-cut wealth, not a growth in our capital stock of happiness, but are merely reparation for the losses it causes. This hyperactivity in general existence tires and weakens

* From *Division of Labor in Society*, pp. 336–42, 345–49.

our nervous system so that we need reparation sufficient to recoup our losses, that is, we need more varied and sophisticated types of satisfaction. Accordingly it becomes even clearer that civilization cannot realistically be made the aim and purpose of the division of labor. Rather is civilization merely a backlash. Civilization can explain neither the existence nor the advances of the division of labor since no inherent and absolute value inheres in it. Rather, on the contrary, civilization has a basis for existence only to the extent that the division of labor is itself found to be indispensable.

No surprise will be forthcoming at the importance thus assigned to the numerical factor if note is taken of the wholly impressive role this factor plays in the historical development of organisms. What characterizes the living being is its two-fold capacity to feed itself and to reproduce itself. But reproduction itself is dependent upon nutrition. Consequently, the intensity of organic life is directly proportional (other things being equal) to nutritive activity, that is, to the number of things an organism can take in. But the appearance of complex organisms has not only been made possible but inevitable because under certain conditions simpler organisms are grouped together so that they form larger aggregations. To the extent that the number of parts making up members of the animal kingdom become more numerous the relations among the parts cease to be stationary, the conditions of social life undergo change and these changes in turn are the determining factors both of the division of labor, and of polymorphism, and of the concentration of living powers and of their expanded energy. Increase in organic substance is accordingly the dominant factor in all zoolgical development. It is not surprising that social development should be subject to the same principle.

Yet even without recourse to reasoning by analogy, it is not difficult to explain the basic role of this numerical factor. All social life rests on a system of facts emanating from direct and long-standing relationships that have been established among many individuals. Hence social life becomes more intense to the extent that the interactions among the component units themselves become more frequent and dynamic. Now, what do this frequency and dynamism depend on? On the character of the elements present, on their greater or lesser strength? But . . . individuals are far more a product of a common life than its determinant. If from each is taken away all that is ascribable to the work of society the residue left is not only small but not very varied in its several manifestations. The differences separating individuals would be inexplicable were it not for the diversity of social conditions on which they depend. Therefore we must not search for the cause of the unequal development of societies in the unequal capacities of men. Might this difference in social development be rooted in the unequal longevity of these social relations? But time by itself produces nothing. Time is merely necessary for the eventual appearance of latent energies. Social development rests therefore on no other variable factor than the number of individuals in relationship and their material and moral closeness, that is, on the volume and density of society. The more numerous individuals are and the more closely they interact, the more powerfully and quickly they react—the more intense, therefore, social life becomes. Now it is just this intensification which goes to make up civilization.

Yet even though civilization is an effect of inevitable causes, it can still become a goal, a desirable achievement, in short, an ideal. In every society there is indeed at each period in its history a specific intensity of collective life which is normal in the light of the quantity and distribution of social units. If all goes normally, this situation will assuredly be spontaneously brought about. But the rub is that things cannot be automatically made to come about normally. Health is part of nature but so is illness. For societies as for individual organisms health is only an ideal type which is never entirely realized. Each individual has more or less of these healthy characteristics but nobody has all of them. To try to bring society as close as possible to this degree of perfection is therefore a goal worth pursuing.

Furthermore, the path by which this goal may be reached can be shortened. If reason steps in to lead the way to this goal, rather than permitting causes to engender their effects at random and to follow the forces working on them, it can spare men much heartache. The development of the individual follows that of the species but in a modified way. The individual does not pass through all the stages the species did; some the individual omits entirely, others it traverses more quickly because collective experiences help to speed its passage through them. Now, reason can achieve analogous results. Reason too involves the use of previous experience in order to adapt easily to future experience. Reason, however, involves more than scientific knowledge of ends and means. Sociology in its present status is hardly in a position to lead us successfully to a solution of such practical problems. But beyond the world of clear-cut ideas inhabited by scientists, there is a world of indistinct ideas containing tendencies.

For desire to impel will it need not be enlightened by science. Unclear presentiments suffice to make men feel that they are lacking something, to stimulate ambition, and to lead them simultaneously to perceive where they ought to bend their energies.

Hence a mechanistic view of society does not rule out ideals. Erroneously is such a view taxed with reducing man to the role of inactive spectator of his own history. What is an ideal anyhow if not an anticipation of the achievement of a desirable goal whose attainment is possible precisely because of this anticipation? Because things behave according to laws does not mean that we have nothing to do. Such an objective may be thought petty, requiring merely that we attain a state of health. But that judgment would overlook the fact that for an educated man health consists in the continuous satisfaction of the highest desires as well as other desires; the former no less than the latter are graven in his character. To be sure, such an ideal is not distant and the horizons it opens up are not at all limitless. It would never require raising the powers of society high above us but rather would it require our developing them within a scope set by the actual state of the social environment. All excess, like all poverty, is an evil. What other ideal can indeed be held out? To aim for a civilization beyond that made possible by the nexus of the surrounding environment will result in unloosing sickness into the very society we live in. Collective activity cannot be encouraged beyond the point set by the condition of the social organism without undermining health. Indeed, in every epoch there exists a peculiar refinement of civilization whose sickly character is manifested in a restlessness and an accompanying uneasiness. But such ill-health is never desirable at all.

But though the ideal is always definite it is never definitive. Since progress is a result of changes occurring in the social environment, there is no reason to expect it will ever end. For that to happen the environment would at some given moment have to become stationary. Now such an hypothesis runs contrary to all sound evidence. As long as there are independent societies the number of social units in each of them will necessarily vary. Even if the level of births ever should remain constant there will always be population movements from country to country, either through violent conquest or through slow and quiet infiltration. Indeed, stronger peoples must seek to take over weaker ones just as the more populous spill over into the less populous. Such regularity in the mechanics of social equilibrium is no less necessary than that in the equilibrium of liquids. For any other result it would be necessary for all human societies to have the same dynamic force and the same density. This is inconceivable if only because of the diversity of geographical environment.

True, this source of variation would be wiped out if all humanity formed one single identical society. But aside from our not knowing that such an ideal is capable of realization, it would still be necessary in order for progress to be halted that within this gigantic society the relations between social units be all equally subject to change. They would have to remain forever distributed in the same way. Not only would the total population but also each of its sub-divisions would have to stay numerically fixed. But the very fact that these sub-divisions do not have the same dimensions nor the same force makes such uniformity impossible. Population cannot be concentrated everywhere in the same way. Thus inevitably the largest cities where life is most intense exercise on other areas an attraction proportionate to their importance. Accordingly the migrations which occur end up by concentrating still more social units in special regions and consequently set going there additional progress which slowly spreads out from the innovating points to the rest of the country. Furthermore, these changes radiate still others into the avenues of communication which in turn stimulate still others so that it becomes impossible to stipulate where the repercussions will cease. In short, societies in their process of development not only do not reach a stationary state but, on the contrary, become more mobile and malleable.

. . . . .

Individuals, just like societies, undergo changes in accordance with the changes occurring in the number of social units and their interactions.

First of all, human individuals are gradually freed from total dependence upon biology. An animal is almost wholly hemmed in by the physical environment; its biological structure predetermines its life. Man, on the contrary, is a creature of social forces. To be sure, there are societies of animals but being highly circumscribed, collective life in them is exceedingly simple. Collective life in these societies is also changeless since equilibrium is inevitably stable in such small societies. For these two reasons collective life is easily incarnated in the organism; it not only has roots there but indeed it envelops everything so completely that nothing has its own specific characteristics. Collective life operates through a system of instincts, reflexes not basically different from those operating in organic life. These instincts, to be sure, are peculiar in leading the individual to adapt to the social environment rather than to the physical environment and in being energized by occurrences relative to the common life. However, they are no different basically from those which in other cases determine without previous training the necessary movements for flight and walking. The situation here is wholly different with man since human societies are far more extensive; even the smallest known human societies are more extensive than the majority of animal societies. Being more complex, human societies are also in greater flux. This combination of complexity and change causes human social life to escape constriction into a biological mould. Even where it is most simple it retains this special characteristic. Everywhere there are beliefs and practices common to men that are not ingrained in their bodies. But this phenomenon becomes more apparent in so far as social substance and density have grown. The more people in relationship and the greater their interaction, the more does the resultant of these associations and interactions reach beyond the organism. Man accordingly is subject to causes *sui generis* and their part in making up human nature becomes ever greater.

Moreover, the influence of this social factor grows not alone in relative value but also in absolute value. The same force that enlarges the importance of collective life subverts the organic environment in such a way as to make it more subject to the influence of social forces, thus subordinating it to collective life. Because there are more individuals living together common life is richer and more varied. But to make this variety possible the organic element must be less definite and must be capable of diversification. We have seen clearly that hereditary tendencies and aptitudes have steadily become more general and indefinite; consequently they are more resistant to subordination to instinct. Thus there eventuates a phenomenon completely inverse to that seen at the early stages of evolution. Among animals the organism encompasses social facts and by divesting them of their peculiar characteristic it transforms them into biological facts. Social life is made into material life. With man, on the other hand, and especially in higher societies, social forces take the place of organic forces. The organism is spiritualized.

With this reversal of cause and effect the individual is metamorphosed. Since this activity which induces the peculiar action of social forces cannot be rooted in the organism a new life, also *sui generis*, is superimposed on that of the body. Freer, more complex, escaping the power of the organs underlying it, its distinguishing characteristics become ever more evident as it progresses and insinuates itself. This description recalls the essential traits of psychic life. It undoubtedly would be an exaggeration to hold that psychic life begins only with societies. Yet surely it becomes extensive only with the development of societies. Hence, as has often been noted, the progress of mind is in inverse ratio to that of instinct. Nevertheless mind does not dissolve instinct. As a product of experiences accumulated over generations, instinct has far too great power of resistance to vanish just because it emerges as consciousness. What truly occurs is that mind inhabits only those areas left vacant by instinct or those where instinct cannot obtain a hold. Mind does not make instinct disappear; it simply fills the space instinct leaves open. Moreover, the cause for the retreat of instinct rather than its proportional advance with the advance of life in general lies in the greater influence of the social factor. Hence the great difference separating man from animal, that is, the very great development of his psychic life, comes down to this cause: his very great capacity for social life. In order to understand why psychic functions have from the earliest beginnings of the human species attained a degree of perfection unknown in animal species requires knowledge of how men have been led to form rather vast societies instead of living alone or in small groups. If, as the classical definition goes, man is a reasoning animal it is because he is an associative animal or at least far more associative than other animals.[2]

There is additional support for this view. As long as societies are restricted in size and in density the only psychic life capable of being developed is one common to all members of the group and identical in each member. But as societies become large and especially as they become dense a psychic life of a new sort makes its appearance. Individual differences, originally lacking or indistinguishable amidst the bulk of social likenesses, appear in bold relief and increase. A host of things that had persisted beyond the reach of individual minds because they were of no concern to collective life become objects of representations. Individuals had been behaving in obligatory fashion towards each other except where their conduct was determined by physical needs but now each one of them becomes an

[2] DeQuatrefages' definition according to which man is a religious animal is a special case of his being an associative animal since man's religious proclivity is a consequence of his outstanding associative capacity.

agent for spontaneous activity. Special types of personality come forth and become self-conscious. Yet this growth of individual psychic life does not weaken society's but merely transforms it. The collective psychic life becomes freer and wider; having by definition no other base except in individual minds, it involves their widening, their sophistication and their flexibility.

Thus the force which brought forth the differences separating man from animals is the same as that which has impelled man to raise himself ever onward and upward. The steadily growing distance between primitive and civilized man has no other source. The power of ideation slowly emerges from original inchoate feeling, man learns to think conceptually and formulate laws, his mind takes in larger and larger parts of space and time, he becomes discontent with tradition and progressively seeks to control the future, his emotions and strivings which were originally few and simple increase and diversify —all these events occur because the social environment has changed continuously. In short, either these changes are created in a vacuum or they have been brought about by corresponding changes in surrounding environments. Now, man is dependent upon three kinds of environment: the body, the external world, society. Except for those accidental variations emanating from new hereditary strains, whose part in human progress is very small, there is no change that occurs in the human organism in and of itself. It must be forced to change by some outside cause. The physical world has since the dawn of history remained basically the same except for innovations introduced by society.[3] Consequently, only society has changed to a degree sufficient to explain the parallel changes in the character of individuals.

No brashness is any longer involved in pronouncing that despite the progress made by physiological psychology it can never encompass more than a minor part of psychology as a whole since the major part of psychic phenomena do not come from organic causes. Philosophers of idealism have always understood this situation and they have rendered a great service to science by combatting all doctrines that reduce psychic life to nothing more than an efflorescence of physical life. They felt most properly that psychic life in its highest manifestations is much too free and complex to be merely an elongation of physical life. But because psychic life is in some part independent of

[3] Transformations of the soil and of streams through the art of husbandry, through engineering, etc.

the biological organism does not mean that it is independent of natural causes and must be considered apart from nature. Rather do all these facts that are unexplained by biological structure depend upon characteristics of the social environment. At least this hypothesis assumes exceedingly great likelihood from the preceding discussion. Now, the social realm is just as natural as the organic realm. Consequently, it is not to be inferred that because there is a vast region of mind whose growth is inexplicable by physiological psychology alone that it must be self-generative and therefore impervious to scientific investigation. Rather does it require a different positive science that should be called social psychology. The phenomena that constitute its subject-matter must inevitably be of a mixed sort: they have the same essential characteristics as other psychic facts but they rest on social causes.

5

Social Normality

The normality of a social fact can only be judged, according to Durkheim, in relation to the type of society in which it occurs and the phase of that society's development. It can be adjudged normal if it is both general in the society and inextricably tied in with the "general conditions of the social type considered." Moreover, what leads to ascribing abnormality to a social fact may be only an embryonic form of it on its way to mature growth.

At the time Durkheim wrote on normality in the Rules, he was much taken with biological analogies. The same is true when he wrestled in the Division of Labor in Society and in Suicide with the problem of abnormal types of those phenomena specifically.

Durkheim moved about with the concept of normality. His criterion of "generality" really betokens a statistical interpretation of normality as the average, the modal case of which there are more than of any other type of case. On the other hand, when he calls crime normal, he does so through a limiting concept of normal. Thus in his view a rate of crime is normal when it is consonant with a type of society at a given phase of its development "provided that it attains and does not exceed, for each social type, a certain level. . . ." Yet sometimes Durkheim seems to set the ideal as the normal—a social criterion for judgment of how men live up to their verbalized values as enshrined for example in laws.

Durkheim holds that a certain amount of suicide is to be expected in any society, particularly in special environments where collective states of egoism, altruism, or anomy are strong. As accentuated in these special environments they may be abnormal states leading to high rates of egoistic suicide or of altruistic suicide or of anomic suicide. He writes: "When a state is said to be normal or abnormal, one must add, 'With reference to this or that,' or else one is misunderstood."

Durkheim looks at suicide rates and crime rates as indicators of normality. In modern psychoanalytic theory, however, a criminal and a suicidal potential is held to be universal in man. In the light of that theory it may be asked: What emotional factors relative to what social factors restrain people from committing suicide or crime? The involved nuances of behavior revealed by psychoanalysis lead beyond Durkheim, although he might have penetrated them if this psychological method had been at his disposal.

The Concept of Social Normality*

. . . We may . . . formulate the three following rules:

1. A social fact is normal, in relation to a given social type at a given phase of its development, when it is present in the average society of that species at the corresponding phase of its evolution.

2. One can verify the results of the preceding method by showing that the generality of the phenomenon is bound up with the general conditions of collective life of the social type considered.

3. This verification is necessary when the fact in question occurs in a social species which has not yet reached the full course of its evolution.

Crime and Normality†

If there is any fact whose pathological character appears incontestable, that fact is crime. . . . But let us see if this problem does not demand a more extended consideration.

We shall apply the foregoing rules. Crime is present not only in

* From *The Rules of Sociological Method*, p. 64.
† From *The Rules of Sociological Method*, pp. 65–67, 70, 71, 72, 74–75.

the majority of societies of one particular species but in all societies
of all types. There is no society that is not confronted with the
problem of criminality. Its form changes; the acts thus characterized
are not the same everywhere; but, everywhere and always, there have
been men who have behaved in such a way as to draw upon themselves penal repression. . . . There is, then, no phenomenon that
presents more indisputably all the symptoms of normality, since it
appears closely connected with the conditions of all collective life.
To make of crime a form of social morbidity would be to admit that
morbidity is not something accidental, but, on the contrary, that in
certain cases it grows out of the fundamental constitution of the
living organism; it would result in wiping out all distinction between
the physiological and the pathological. No doubt it is possible that
crime itself will have abnormal forms, as, for example, when its rate
is unusually high. This excess is, indeed, undoubtedly morbid in
nature. What is normal, simply, is the existence of criminality, provided that it attains and does not exceed, for each social type, a certain
level, which it is perhaps not impossible to fix in conformity with
the preceding rules.[1]

                    .   .   .   .   .

In the first place crime is normal because a society exempt from it
is utterly impossible. . . .

                    .   .   .   .   .

Crime is . . . bound up with the fundamental conditions of all
social life, and by that very fact it is useful, because these conditions
of which it is a part are themselves indispensable to the normal
evolution of morality and law.

                    .   .   .   .   .

. . . . Aside from this indirect utility, it happens that crime itself
plays a useful role in this evolution. Crime implies not only that the
way remains open to necessary changes but that in certain cases it
directly prepares these changes. Where crime exists, collective sentiments are sufficiently flexible to take on a new form, and crime sometimes helps to determine the form they will take. How many times,

[1] From the fact that crime is a phenomenon of normal sociology, it does not follow that the criminal is an individual normally constituted from the biological and
psychological points of view. The two questions are independent of each other.
This independence will be better understood when we have shown, later on, the
difference between psychological and sociological facts.

indeed, is it only an anticipation of future morality—a step toward what will be! . . .

. . . . .

From this point of view the fundamental facts of criminality present themselves to us in an entirely new light. Contrary to current ideas, the criminal no longer seems a totally unsociable being, a sort of parasitic element, a strange and unassimilable body, introduced into the midst of society. On the contrary, he plays a definite role in social life. Crime, for its part, must no longer be conceived as an evil that cannot be too much suppressed. . . .

. . . . .

The principal object of all sciences of life, whether individual or social, is to define and explain the normal state and to distinguish it from its opposite. If, however, normality is not given in the things themselves—if it is, on the contrary, a character we may or may not impute to them—this solid footing is lost. The mind is then complacent in the face of a reality which has little to teach it; it is no longer restrained by the matter which it is analyzing, since it is the mind, in some manner or other, that determines the matter.

The various principles we have established up to the present are, then, closely interconnected. In order that sociology may be a true science of things, the generality of phenomena must be taken as the criterion of their normality.

Our method has, moreover, the advantage of regulating action at the same time as thought. If the social values are not subjects of observation but can and must be determined by a sort of mental calculus, no limit, so to speak, can be set for the free inventions of the imagination in search of the best. For how may we assign to perfection a limit? It escapes all limitation, by definition. The goal of humanity recedes into infinity, discouraging some by its very remoteness and arousing others who, in order to draw a little nearer to it, quicken the pace and plunge into revolutions. This practical dilemma may be escaped if the desirable is defined in the same way as is health and normality and if health is something that is defined as inherent in things. For then the object of our efforts is both given and defined at the same time. It is no longer a matter of pursuing desperately an objective that retreats as one advances, but of working with steady perseverance to maintain the normal state, of re-establishing it if it is threatened, and of rediscovering its conditions if they have changed. The duty of the statesman is no longer to push society toward an ideal that seems attractive to him, but his role is that of the physician: he prevents the outbreak of illnesses by good hygiene, and he seeks to cure them when they have appeared.[2]

Contemporary Suicide and Normality[*]

. . . Should the present state of suicide among civilized peoples be considered as normal or abnormal? According to the solution one adopts, he will consider reforms necessary and possible with a view to restraining it, or, on the contrary, will agree, not without censure, to accept it as it is.

Some are perhaps astonished that this question could be raised.

It is true, we usually regard everything immoral as abnormal. Therefore, if suicide offends the public conscience, as has been established, it seems impossible not to see in it a phenomenon of social pathology. But we have shown elsewhere[3] that even the preeminent form of immorality, crime itself, need not necessarily be classed among morbid manifestations. . . .

. . . . .

Let us apply these ideas to suicide.

We have not sufficient data, it is true, to be sure that there is no society where suicide is not found. Statistics on suicide are available to us for only a small number of peoples. For the rest, the existence of chronic suicide can be proved only by the traces it leaves in legislation. Now, we do not know with certainty that suicide has everywhere been the object of juridical regulation. But we may affirm that this is usually the case. It is sometimes proscribed, sometimes reproved; sometimes its interdiction is formal, sometimes it includes reserva-

---

[2] From the theory developed in this chapter, the conclusion has at times been reached that, according to us, the increase of criminality in the course of the nineteenth century was a normal phenomenon. Nothing is farther from our thought. Several facts indicated by us apropos of suicide tend, on the contrary, to make us believe that this development is in general morbid. Nevertheless, it might happen that a certain increase of certain forms of criminality would be normal, for each state of civilization has its own criminality. But on this, one can only formulate hypotheses.

[3] See *Rules of Sociological Method*, ch. 3.

[*] From *Suicide*, pp. 361, 363–66.

tions and exceptions. But all analogies permit the belief that it can never have remained a matter of indifference to law and morality; that is, it has always been sufficiently important to attract the attention of the public conscience. At any rate, it is certain that suicido-genetic currents of different intensity, depending on the historical period, have always existed among the peoples of Europe; statistics prove it ever since the last century, and juridical monuments prove it for earlier periods. Suicide is therefore an element of their normal constitution, and even, probably, of any social constitution.

It is also possible to see their mutual connection.

This is especially true of altruistic suicide with respect to lower societies. Precisely because the strict subordination of the individual to the group is the principle on which they rest, altruistic suicide is there, so to speak, an indispensable procedure of their collective discipline. If men, there, did not set a low value on life, they would not be what they should be; and from the moment they value it so lightly, everything inevitably becomes a pretext for them to abandon it. So there is a close connection between the practice of this sort of suicide and the moral organization of this sort of society. It is the same today in those special settings where abnegation and impersonality are essential. Even now, military esprit can only be strong if the individual is self-detached, and such detachment necessarily throws the door open to suicide.

For opposite reasons, in societies and environments where the dignity of the person is the supreme end of conduct, where man is a God to mankind, the individual is readily inclined to consider the man in himself as a God and to regard himself as the object of his own cult. When morality consists primarily in giving one a very high idea of one's self, certain combinations of circumstances readily suffice to make man unable to perceive anything above himself. Individualism is of course not necessarily egoism, but it comes close to it; the one cannot be stimulated without the other being enlarged. Thus, egoistic suicide arises. Finally, among peoples where progress is and should be rapid, rules restraining individuals must be sufficiently pliable and malleable; if they preserved all the rigidity they possess in primitive societies, evolution thus impeded could not take place promptly enough. But then inevitably, under weaker restraint, desires and ambitions overflow impetuously at certain points. As soon as men are inoculated with the precept that their duty is to progress, it is harder to make them accept resignation; so the number of the malcontent and disquieted is bound to increase. The entire morality of progress and perfection is thus inseparable from a certain amount of anomy. Hence, a definite moral constitution corresponds to each type of suicide and is interconnected with it. One cannot exist without the other, for suicide is only the form inevitably assumed by each moral constitution under certain conditions, particular, to be sure, but inescapably arising.

We shall be answered that these varied currents cause suicide only if exaggerated; and asked whether they might not have everywhere a single, moderate intensity? This is wishing for the conditions of life to be everywhere the same, which is neither possible nor desirable. There are special environments in every society which are reached by collective states only through the latter being modified; according to circumstances, they are strengthened or weakened. For a current to have a certain strength in most of the country, it therefore has to exceed or fail to reach this strength at certain points.

But not only are these excesses in one or the other direction necessary; they have their uses. For if the most general state is also the one best adapted to the most general circumstances of social life, it cannot be so related with unusual circumstances; yet society must be capable of being adapted to both. A man in whom the taste for activity never surpassed the average could not maintain himself in situations requiring an unusual effort. Likewise, a society in which intellectual individualism could not be exaggerated would be unable to shake off the yoke of tradition and renew its faiths, even when this became necessary. Inversely, where this same spiritual state could not on occasion be reduced enough to allow the opposite current to develop, what would happen in time of war, when passive obedience is the highest duty? But, for these forms of activity to be produced when they are needed, society must not have totally forgotten them. Thus, it is indispensable that they have a place in the common existence; there must be circles where an unrelenting spirit of criticism and free examination is maintained, others, like the army, where the old religion of authority is preserved almost intact. Of course, in ordinary times, the influence of these special foci must be restricted to certain limits; since the sentiments which flourish there relate to particular circumstances, they must not be generalized. But if they must remain localized, it is equally important that they exist. This need will seem still clearer if we remember that societies not only are required to confront different situations in the course of a single period, but that they cannot even endure without transformation. Within one century, the normal proportions of individualism and altruism fitting for modern peoples will no longer be the same. But the future would be impossible if its germs were not contained in the present. For a collective tendency to be able to grow weaker or stronger through evolution, it must not become set once for all in a single form, from which it could not free itself; it could not vary in time if it were incapable of variation in space.[4]

The different currents of collective sadness which derive from these three moral states have their own reasons for existence so long as they are not excessive. Indeed, it is wrong to believe that unmixed joy is the normal state of sensibility. Man could not live if he were entirely impervious to sadness. Many sorrows can be endured only by being embraced, and the pleasure taken in them naturally has a somewhat melancholy character. So, melancholy is morbid only when it occupies too much place in life; but it is equally morbid for it to be wholly excluded from life. The taste for happy expansiveness must be moderated by the opposite taste; only on this condition will it retain measure and harmonize with reality. It is the same with societies as with individuals. Too cheerful a morality is a loose morality; it is appropriate only to decadent peoples and is found only among them. Life is often harsh, treacherous or empty. Collective sensibility must reflect this side of existence, too. This is why there has to be, beside the current of optimism which impels men to regard the world confidently, an opposite current, less intense, of course, and less general than the first, but able to restrain it partially; for a tendency does not limit itself, it can never be restrained except by another tendency. From certain indications it even seems that the tendency to a sort of melancholy develops as we rise in the scale of social types. As we have said in another work, it is a quite remarkable fact that the great religions of the most civilized peoples are more deeply fraught with sadness than the simpler beliefs of earlier societies. This certainly does not mean that the current of pessimism is eventually

[4] What helps make this question unclear is the failure to observe how relative these ideas of sickness and health are. What is normal today will no longer be so tomorrow, and vice versa. The large intestines of primitive man are normal for his environment but would not be so today. What is morbid for individuals may be normal for society. Neurasthenia is a sickness from the point of view of individual physiology; but what would a society be without neurasthenics? They really have a social role to play. When a state is said to be normal or abnormal, one must add, "With reference to this or that," or else one is misunderstood.

to submerge the other, but it proves that it does not lose ground and that it does not seem destined to disappear. Now, for it to exist and maintain itself, there must be a special organ in society to serve as its substratum. There must be groups of individuals who more especially represent this aspect of the collective mood. But the part of the population which plays this role is necessarily that where ideas of suicide easily take root.

6

Modern Social Pathology
and Anomy

Durkheim was especially concerned about abnormal forms of behavior in modern western society, particularly about abnormal forms of the division of labor and about suicide as an abnormal form of modern individualism.

Suicide is found in every type of society and some instances of it must be expected, but Durkheim holds that the suicide rate had become abnormal at the close of the nineteenth century in Europe, particularly in certain special environments and especially in those markedly Protestant. He claims that the high rate of suicide at the end of the nineteenth century springs from a social pathology. This pathological state has its basis in discontent, a discontent triggered by the search for money and goods in the economic sphere that leads to expectations of fulfillment beyond the capacity of even riches to achieve. Riches instead of appeasing appetites increase them beyond the point of possible satisfaction. Sudden economic depressions throw the nouveaux riches into emotional depressions that lead to suicide. Anomic suicide viewed collectively gives evidence of the absence of regulation of individual appetites; viewed from the standpoint of the individual it is the haunting search for the unattainable.

The anomic forms of the division of labor, on the other hand, involve breakdowns of social cohesion and solidarity arising from lack of clear and consistent regulation. The three types of anomy relative to the division of labor involve: (1) industrial and commercial crises; (2) the conflict between capital and labor; and (3) the overrefined division of labor, which separates scientists from each other to such a point as to endanger the unity of science.

Durkheim's concept of anomy is an ingenious one. His use of it in Suicide comes within reach of psychoanalysis, which has done so much since Durkheim's time to enlighten us on the phenomenon of self-destruction.*

As already noted in the introduction to this book, in recent decades some American sociologists have been promiscuously applying the concept of anomy to every social problem and every instance of social disorganization so that it has come to mean almost nothing through being made to mean everything. It is well to turn to Durkheim's own discussions and keep from doing him the injustice of making the concept of anomy a maid of all work.

Suicide and Social Pathology†

. . . It does not follow from the fact that a suicidogenetic current of a certain strength must be considered as a phenomenon of normal sociology, that every current of the same sort is necessarily of the same character. If the spirit of renunciation, the love of progress, the taste for individuation have their place in every kind of society, and cannot exist without becoming generators of suicide at certain points, it is further necessary for them to have this property only in a certain measure, varying with various peoples. It is only justified if it does not pass certain limits. Likewise, the collective penchant for sadness is only wholesome as long as it is not preponderant. So the above remarks have not settled the question whether the present status of suicide among civilized nations is or is not normal. We need further to consider whether its tremendous aggravation during the past century is not pathological in origin.

It has been called the ransom-money of civilization. Certainly, it is general in Europe and more pronounced the higher the culture of European nations. . . .

. . . This aggravation springs not from the intrinsic nature of

* I have sought in my introduction to the English translation of Durkheim's *Suicide* to bring his view and that of psychoanalysis within hailing distance of each other. The reader is referred to that introduction for further details.
† From *Suicide*, pp. 366–67, 368–70.

progress but from the special conditions under which it occurs in our day, and nothing assures us that these conditions are normal. For we must not be dazzled by the brilliant development of sciences, the arts and industry of which we are the witnesses; this development is altogether certainly taking place in the midst of a morbid effervescence, the grievous repercussions of which each one of us feels. It is then very possible and even probable that the rising tide of suicide originates in a pathological state just now accompanying the march of civilization without being its necessary condition.

The rapidity of the growth of suicides really permits no other hypothesis. Actually, in less than fifty years, they have tripled, quadrupled, and even quintupled, depending on the country. On the other hand, we know their connection with the most ineradicable element in the constitution of societies, since they express the mood of societies, and since the mood of peoples, like that of individuals, reflects the state of the most fundamental part of the organism. Our social organization, then, must have changed profoundly in the course of this century, to have been able to cause such a growth in the suicide-rate. So grave and rapid an alteration as this must be morbid; for a society cannot change its structure so suddenly. Only by a succession of slow, almost imperceptible modifications does it achieve different characteristics. The possible changes, even then, are limited. Once a social type is fixed it is no longer infinitely plastic; a limit is soon reached which cannot be passed. Thus the changes presupposed by the statistics of contemporary suicides cannot be normal. Without even knowing exactly of what they consist, we may begin by affirming that they result not from a regular evolution but from a morbid disturbance which, while able to uproot the institutions of the past, has put nothing in their place; for the work of centuries cannot be remade in a few years. But if the cause is so abnormal, the effect must be so, as well. Thus, what the rising flood of voluntary deaths denotes is not the increasing brilliancy of our civilization but a state of crisis and perturbation not to be prolonged with impunity.

To these various reasons another may be added. Though it is true that collective sadness has, normally, a role to play in the life of societies, it is not ordinarily general or intense enough to reach the higher centers of the social body. It remains a submerged current, felt vaguely by the collective personality, which therefore undergoes its influence without clearly taking it into account. At least, if these, vague dispositions do affect the common conscience, it is only by tentative and intermittent thrusts. Generally they are expressed merely by fragmentary judgments, isolated maxims, unrelated to one another and which, in spite of their intransigent aspect, are intended to convey only one side of reality, to be corrected and supplemented by contradictory maxims. Thence come the melancholy sayings and proverbial sallies at life's expense in which sometimes is put the wisdom of nations, but without being more frequent than their opposite numbers. Clearly they convey passing impressions, which have transiently touched consciousness without taking full possession of it. Only when such sentiments acquire unusual strength do they sufficiently absorb public attention to be seen as a whole, coordinated and systematized, and then become the bases of complete theories of life. In fact, in Rome and in Greece, it was when society felt itself seriously endangered that the discouraging theories of Epicurus and Zeno appeared. The formation of such great systems is therefore an indication that the current of pessimism has reached a degree of abnormal intensity which is due to some disturbance of the social organism. We well know how these systems have recently multiplied. To form a true idea of their number and importance it is not enough to consider the philosophies avowedly of this nature, such as those of Schopenhauer, Hartmann, etc. We must also consider all the others which derive from the same spirit under different names. The anarchist, the aesthete, the mystic, the socialist revolutionary, even if they do not despair of the future, have in common with the pessimist a single sentiment of hatred and disgust for the existing order, a single craving to destroy or to escape from reality. Collective melancholy would not have penetrated consciousness so far, if it had not undergone a morbid development; and so the development of suicide resulting from it is of the same nature.

All proofs combine therefore to make us consider the enormous increase in the number of voluntary deaths within a century as a pathological phenomenon becoming daily a greater menace. . . .

The Meaning of Anomy
and of Anomic Suicide*

No living being can be happy or even exist unless his needs are sufficiently proportioned to his means. In other words, if his needs require more than can be granted, or even merely something of a different sort, they will be under continual friction and can only function painfully. Movements incapable of production without pain tend not to be reproduced. Unsatisfied tendencies atrophy, and as the impulse to live is merely the result of all the rest, it is bound to weaken as the others relax.

In the animal, at least in a normal condition, this equilibrium is established with automatic spontaneity because the animal depends on purely material conditions. . . .

This is not the case with man, because most of his needs are not dependent on his body or not to the same degree. Strictly speaking, we may consider that the quantity of material supplies necessary to the physical maintenance of a human life is subject to computation, though this be less exact than in the preceding case and a wider margin left for the free combinations of the will; for beyond the indispensable minimum which satisfies nature when instinctive, a more awakened reflection suggests better conditions, seemingly desirable ends craving fulfillment. Such appetites, however, admittedly sooner or later reach a limit which they cannot pass. But how determine the quantity of well-being, comfort or luxury legitimately to be craved by a human being? Nothing appears in man's organic nor in his psychological constitution which sets a limit to such tendencies. The functioning of individual life does not require them to cease at one point rather than at another; the proof being that they have constantly increased since the beginnings of history, receiving more and more complete satisfaction, yet with no weakening of average health. Above all, how establish their proper variation with different conditions of life, occupations, relative importance of services, etc.? In no society are they equally satisfied in the different stages of the

* From *Suicide*, pp. 246, 247–49, 250–51, 252–54, 256, 257–58.

social hierarchy. Yet human nature is substantially the same among all men, in its essential qualities. It is not human nature which can assign the variable limits necessary to our needs. They are thus unlimited so far as they depend on the individual alone. Irrespective of any external regulatory force, our capacity for feeling is in itself an insatiable and bottomless abyss.

But if nothing external can restrain this capacity, it can only be a source of torment to itself. Unlimited desires are insatiable by definition and insatiability is rightly considered a sign of morbidity. Being unlimited, they constantly and infinitely surpass the means at their command; they cannot be quenched. Inextinguishable thirst is constantly renewed torture. It has been claimed, indeed, that human activity naturally aspires beyond assignable limits and sets itself unattainable goals. But how can such an undetermined state be any more reconciled with the conditions of mental life than with the demands of physical life? All man's pleasure in acting, moving and exerting himself implies the sense that his efforts are not in vain and that by walking he has advanced. However, one does not advance when one walks toward no goal, or—which is the same thing—when his goal is infinity. . . . But it would be a miracle if no insurmountable obstacle were never encountered. Our thread of life on these conditions is pretty thin, breakable at any instant.

To achieve any other result, the passions first must be limited. Only then can they be harmonized with the faculties and satisfied. But since the individual has no way of limiting them, this must be done by some force exterior to him. A regulative force must play the same role for moral needs which the organism plays for physical needs. This means that the force can only be moral. The awakening of conscience interrupted the state of equilibrium of the animal's dormant existence; only conscience, therefore, can furnish the means to re-establish it. Physical restraint would be ineffective; hearts cannot be touched by physio-chemical forces. So far as the appetites are not automatically restrained by physiological mechanisms, they can be halted only by a limit that they recognize as just. Men would never consent to restrict their desires if they felt justified in passing the assigned limit. But, for reasons given above, they cannot assign themselves this law of justice. So they must receive it from an authority which they respect, to which they yield spontaneously. Either directly and as a whole, or through the agency of one of its organs, society alone can play this moderating role; for it is the only moral power superior to the individual, the authority of which he accepts. It alone has the power necessary to stipulate law and to set the point beyond which the passions must not go. Finally, it alone can estimate the reward to be prospectively offered to every class of human functionary, in the name of the common interest.

. . . . .

Under this pressure, each in his sphere vaguely realizes the extreme limit set to his ambitions and aspires to nothing beyond. At least if he respects regulations and is docile to collective authority, that is, has a wholesome moral constitution, he feels that it is not well to ask more. Thus, an end and goal are set to the passions. Truly, there is nothing rigid nor absolute about such determination. The economic ideal assigned each class of citizens is itself confined to certain limits, within which the desires have free range. But it is not infinite. This relative limitation and the moderation it involves, make men contented with their lot while stimulating them moderately to improve it; and this average contentment causes the feeling of calm, active happiness, the pleasure in existing and living which characterizes health for societies as well as for individuals. Each person is then at least, generally speaking, in harmony with his condition, and desires only what he may legitimately hope for as the normal reward of his activity. Besides, this does not condemn man to a sort of immobility. He may seek to give beauty to his life; but his attempts in this direction may fail without causing him to despair. For, loving what he has and not fixing his desire solely on what he lacks, his wishes and hopes may fail of what he has happened to aspire to, without his being wholly destitute. He has the essentials. The equilibrium of his happiness is secure because it is defined, and a few mishaps cannot disconcert him.

But it would be of little use for everyone to recognize the justice of the hierarchy of functions established by public opinion, if he did not also consider the distribution of these functions just. The workman is not in harmony with his social position if he is not convinced that he has his desserts. If he feels justified in occupying another, what he has would not satisfy him. So it is not enough for the average level of needs for each social condition to be regulated by public opinion, but another, more precise rule, must fix the way in which these conditions are open to individuals. There is no society in which such regulation does not exist. It varies with times and places. Once it regarded birth as the almost exclusive principle of social classification; today it recognizes no other inherent inequality than hereditary fortune and merit. But in all these various forms its object is unchanged. It is also only possible, everywhere, as a restriction upon individuals imposed by superior authority, that is, by collective authority. For it can be established only by requiring of one or another group of men, usually of all, sacrifices and concessions in the name of the public interest.

. . . . .

It is not true, then, that human activity can be released from all restraint. Nothing in the world can enjoy such a privilege. All existence being a part of the universe is relative to the remainder; its nature and method of manifestation accordingly depend not only on itself but on other beings, who consequently restrain and regulate it. Here there are only differences of degree and form between the mineral realm and the thinking person. Man's characteristic privilege is that the bond he accepts is not physical but moral; that is, social. He is governed not by a material environment brutally imposed on him, but by a conscience superior to his own, the superiority of which he feels. Because the greater, better part of his existence transcends the body, he escapes the body's yoke, but is subject to that of society.

But when society is disturbed by some painful crisis or by beneficent but abrupt transitions, it is momentarily incapable of exercising this influence; thence come the sudden rises in the curve of suicides. . . .

In the case of economic disasters, indeed, something like a declassification occurs which suddenly casts certain individuals into a lower state than their previous one. Then they must reduce their requirements, restrain their needs, learn greater self-control. All the advantages of social influence are lost so far as they are concerned; their moral education has to be recommenced. But society cannot adjust them instantaneously to this new life and teach them to practice the increased self-repression to which they are unaccustomed. So they are not adjusted to the condition forced on them, and its very prospect is intolerable; hence the suffering which detaches them from a reduced existence even before they have made trial of it.

It is the same if the source of the crisis is an abrupt growth of power and wealth. Then, truly, as the conditions of life are changed, the standard according to which needs were regulated can no longer remain the same; for it varies with social resources, since it largely determines the share of each class of producers. The scale is upset;

but a new scale cannot be immediately improvised. Time is required for the public conscience to reclassify men and things. So long as the social forces thus freed have not regained equilibrium, their respective values are unknown and so all regulation is lacking for a time. . . .

. . . . The state of de-regulation or anomy is thus further heightened by passions being less disciplined, precisely when they need more disciplining.

But then their very demands make fulfillment impossible. Overweening ambition always exceeds the results obtained, great as they may be, since there is no warning to pause here. Nothing gives satisfaction and all this agitation is uninteruptedly maintained without appeasement. Above all, since this race for an unattainable goal can give no other pleasure but that of the race itself, if it is one, once it is interrupted the participants are left empty-handed. At the same time the struggle grows more violent and painful, both from being less controlled and because competition is greater. All classes contend among themselves because no established classification any longer exists. Effort grows, just when it becomes less productive. How could the desire to live not be weakened under such conditions?

This explanation is confirmed by the remarkable immunity of poor countries. Poverty protects against suicide because it is a restraint in itself. No matter how one acts, desires have to depend upon resources to some extent; actual possessions are partly the criterion of those aspired to. So the less one has the less he is tempted to extend the range of his needs indefinitely. Lack of power, compelling moderation, accustoms men to it, while nothing excites envy if no one has superfluity. Wealth, on the other hand, by the power it bestows, deceives us into believing that we depend on ourselves only. Reducing the resistance we encounter from objects, it suggests the possibility of unlimited success against them. The less limited one feels, the more intolerable all limitation appears. Not without reason, therefore, have so many religions dwelt on the advantages and moral value of poverty. It is actually the best school for teaching self-restraint. Forcing us to constant self-discipline, it prepares us to accept collective discipline with equanimity, while wealth, exalting the individual, may always arouse the spirit of rebellion which is the very source of immorality. This, of course, is no reason why humanity should not improve its material condition. But though the moral danger involved in every growth of prosperity is not irremediable, it should not be forgotten.

If anomy never appeared except, as in the above instances, in intermittent spurts and acute crisis, it might cause the social suicide-rate
to vary from time to time, but it would not be a regular, constant
factor. In one sphere of social life, however—the sphere of trade and
industry—it is actually in a chronic state.

. . . . . .

. . . . From top to bottom of the ladder, greed is aroused without
knowing where to find ultimate foothold. Nothing can calm it, since
its goal is far beyond all it can attain. Reality seems valueless by
comparison with the dreams of fevered imaginations; reality is therefore abandoned, but so too is possibility abandoned when it in turn
becomes reality. A thirst arises for novelties, unfamiliar pleasures,
nameless sensations, all of which lose their savor once known. Henceforth one has no strength to endure the least reverse. The whole
fever subsides and the sterility of all the tumult is apparent, and it
is seen that all these new sensations in their infinite quantity cannot
form a solid foundation of happiness to support one during days of
trial. The wise man, knowing how to enjoy achieved results without
having constantly to replace them with others, finds in them an
attachment to life in the hour of difficulty. But the man who has
always pinned all his hopes on the future and lived with his eyes fixed
upon it, has nothing in the past as a comfort against the present's
afflictions, for the past was nothing to him but a series of hastily
experienced stages. What blinded him to himself was his expectation
always to find further on the happiness he had so far missed. Now
he is stopped in his tracks; from now on nothing remains behind or
ahead of him to fix his gaze upon. Weariness alone, moreover, is
enough to bring disillusionment, for he cannot in the end escape the
futility of an endless pursuit.

. . . . . .

Industrial and commercial functions are really among the occupations which furnish the greatest number of suicides. Almost on a
level with the liberal professions, they sometimes surpass them; they
are especially more afflicted than agriculture, where the old regulative
forces still make their appearance felt most and where the fever of
business has least penetrated. Here is best recalled what was once the
general constitution of the economic order. And the divergence would
be yet greater if, among the suicides of industry, employers were
distinguished from workmen, for the former are probably most
stricken by the state of anomy. The enormous rate of those with

independent means (720 per million) sufficiently shows that the possessors of most comfort suffer most. Everything that enforces subordination attenuates the effects of this state. At least the horizon of the lower classes is limited by those above them, and for this same reason their desires are more modest. Those who have only empty space above them are almost inevitably lost in it, if no force restrains them.

Anomy, therefore, is a regular and specific factor in suicide in our modern societies; one of the springs from which the annual contingent feeds. So we have here a new type to distinguish from the others. It differs from them in its dependence, not on the way in which individuals are attached to society, but on how it regulates them. Egoistic suicide results from man's no longer finding a basis for existence in life; altruistic suicide, because this basis for existence appears to man situated beyond life itself. The third sort of suicide, the existence of which has just been shown, results from man's activity's lacking regulation and his consequent sufferings. By virtue of its origin we shall assign this last variety the name of *anomic suicide.*

Anomy and the Division of Labor*

. . . We have studied the division of labor . . . as a normal phenomenon but like all social facts and, more generally, all biological facts, it presents pathological forms which must be analyzed. Though normally the division of labor produces social solidarity, it sometimes happens that it has different and even contrary results. Now, it is important to find out what makes it deviate from its natural course since so long as the exceptional character of these cases is not established, the division of labor might be suspected of logically implying them. Moreover, the study of these deviant forms will enable us to determine better the conditions in which the normal state exists. When we know the circumstances in which the division of labor ceases to bring forth solidarity, we shall understand better how it does bring forth solidarity. Pathology, here as elsewhere, is a valuable aid of physiology.

. . . . .

* From *Division of Labor in Society*, pp. 353, 354–57, 368–71.

The first case of this kind is furnished us by industrial or commercial crises, by failures, which are partial ruptures of organic solidarity. They evince, in effect, that at certain points in the organism certain social functions are not adjusted to one another. Now, to the extent that labor is increasingly divided, these phenomena seem to become more frequent, at least in certain cases. From 1845 to 1869 failures increased 70 per cent. We cannot however attribute this fact to the growth in economic life since enterprises have become concentrated rather than more numerous.

The conflict between capital and labor is another and more striking example of the same phenomenon. In so far as industrial functions become more specialized, the conflict, far from leading to greater solidarity, becomes sharper. In the middle ages the worker everywhere lived at the side of his master, sharing the work "in the same shop, at the same workbench." Both were part of the same corporation and led the same existence. "They were on an almost equal footing; whoever had served his apprenticeship could, at least in many of the occupations, set himself up independently if he had the means." Thus conflicts were wholly unusual. Beginning with the fifteenth century things began to change. "The occupation is no longer a common refuge; it is exclusively the possession of the masters, who made all decisions. . . . Henceforth a sharp line is drawn between masters and journeymen. The latter formed, so to speak, an order apart; they had their customs, their rules, their independent associations." Once this separation was effected, quarrels became numerous. "As soon as the journeymen had a complaint, they struck or boycotted a village, an employer, and all were compelled to obey the letter of the order. . . . The power of association gave the workers the means of struggling against their employers on equal terms." At that time, however, things were far from being at "the point where they are now. Journeymen rebelled in order to secure higher wages or some other change in the condition of labor, but they did not consider the employer as a permanent enemy to be obeyed because of force. They wished to make him concede a point, and they went at it vigorously, but the struggle was not everlasting. The workshops did not contain two opposing classes. Our socialist doctrines were unknown." Finally in the seventeenth century, the third phase of this history of the working classes begins: the birth of large-scale industry. The worker is more completely separated from the employer. "He becomes regimented. Each has his function, and the division of labor moves ahead. In the Van-Robais enterprise, which employed 1692 workers, there were special shops for wheel-wrighting, for cutlery, for washing, for dyeing, for warping, and the shops for weaving themselves contained several types of workers whose labor was entirely distinct." At the same time that specialization becomes greater, revolts become more frequent. "The smallest source of discontent was enough to cause an establishment to be boycotted and bring trouble to a journeyman if he did not obey the decree of the group." We know well that the warfare has since become more violent.

To be sure . . . this tension in social relations is due, in part, to the fact that the working classes are not really satisfied with the conditions under which they live but all too often accept them only under constraint and force, since they have no means to change them. This constraint alone, however, would not account for the tension. This tension hits all the poor but the condition of permanent hostility is wholly special to the industrial world. It is the same, without distinction, for all the workers in the industrial world. But small-scale industry, where work is less divided, exhibits a relative harmony between worker and employer. It is only in large-scale industry that this clash is acute. Large-scale industry is therefore to be understood as the source for this type of clash.

Another illustration of the same phenomenon has often been observed in the history of the sciences. Until rather recent times science, being less divided into specialties than it is now, could be cultivated almost entirely by one and the same person. Thus a very keen appreciation of its unity was possible. The particular truths which composed it were neither so numerous nor so heterogeneous that one could not easily see the tie which bound them in one and the same system. Methods, being themselves very general, were little different from one another, and one could perceive the common trunk from which they imperceptibly diverged. But as specialization was introduced into scientific work, each scholar limited himself more and more not only to a particular science but to a special order of problems. Auguste Comte even in his time complained that there were in the scholarly world "very few minds that took in the total scope of even a single science, let alone the totality of all science. Most of them were already entirely occupied by the isolated consideration of a more or less extensive section of one given science without being very much concerned with the relation of their particular labors to the general system of positive knowledge." Hence science, cut up into a multitude of detailed studies not linked together, no longer forms a unified whole. This absence of concert and unity is perhaps best indicated by the widely accepted theory that each particular science has an absolute value and that the scholar ought to devote himself to his special researches without bothering to inquire whether they serve some purpose and lead anywhere. "This division of intellectual labor," says Schaeffle, "offers good reason for fearing that this return to a new Alexandrianism will lead once again to the ruin of all science."

. . . . .

. . . If the division of labor does not produce solidarity in all these cases, it is because the organs are not regulated in orderly fashion, that is, because they are in a state of anomy.

How does this state of anomy come about?

The spontaneously established relations between social functions take the definite form of a body of rules in the course of time. We can say, a priori, therefore, that the state of anomy is impossible wherever solidary organs are sufficiently in contact and have been operative over time. Indeed, being contiguous, they are always readily aware of their mutual dependence; of it they have a vivid and continuous feeling. For the same reason communication among them is easy, frequent, and regular. They coordinate themselves and attain consolidation in time. Finally, since the smallest reaction can be felt from one part to another, the rules which are thus formed carry this interactive imprint; that is to say, they foresee and fix in detail the conditions of equilibrium. But on the contrary, if some opaque milieu is interposed, then only stimuli of a certain intensity can be communicated from one organ to another. The infrequent relations are not repeated sufficiently for consolidation; each new relation must fend for itself. The channels through which communications flow cannot deepen because the communications themselves are intermittent. If some rules do nevertheless come through, they are usually general and vague, for given these conditions phenomena emerge only in their most general contours. The result is the same if contact is sufficient but of insufficient duration.[1]

---

[1] Anomy might occur even when the contact is sufficient and long enough. It might occur when the necessary adaptation can be established only by submitting the social structure to transformations of which it is incapable. The plasticity of societies is not endless. When it reaches its limit, even necessary changes are impossible.

Generally this condition of anomy occurs by the force of these circumstances. A function can be apportioned between two or several parts of an organism only if these parts are more or less contiguous. Moreover, once labor is divided, since the parts need one another, they naturally tend to lessen the distance separating them. That is why as one ascends in the animal scale, the organs become interdependent and, as Spencer says, invade the interstitial areas. But things can turn out differently under exceptional circumstances.

These exceptions occur in the cases we are discussing. In so far as the segmental type is very much in evidence, there are nearly as many economic markets as there are different segments. Consequently, each of them is very limited. Since producers are near consumers, they can easily reckon the extent of the needs to be satisfied. Equilibrium is established without any trouble and production regulates itself. On the other hand, as the organized type develops the fusion of different segments draws the markets together into a single market nearly coterminous with society as a whole. This market even extends further and tends to become universal; the frontiers which separate peoples tend to disappear at the same time as those which separate the segments within each of them. The result is that each industry produces for consumers spread over the whole country or even of the entire world. Contact then is no longer sufficient. The producer can no longer either visualize or comprehend the market. He can no longer see its limits since it is, so to speak, limitless. Accordingly, production goes on unchecked and uncontrolled. It can operate only by trial and error as a result of which overproduction is inevitable in one field or another. From this come the crises which periodically disturb economic functions. The growth of local, restricted crises which result in failures is in all likelihood an effect of the same cause.

As the market expands, big industry appears. It transforms the relations between employers and employees. The needs of the workers increase under nervous fatigue and the contagious influence of urban life. Machines replace men; manufacturing replaces handicraft. The worker is regimented and separated from his family throughout the day. He always lives apart from his employer, etc. These new conditions of industrial life naturally require new organization, but as these changes have occurred with extreme rapidity, the conflicting interests have not yet had the time to reach equilibrium.

Finally, the explanation of the fact that the moral and social sciences are in the state we have suggested is that they were the last to come into the domain of positive sciences. It is hardly a century since this new field of phenomena has been opened to scientific investigation. Scholars have installed themselves in them, some here, some there, according to their tastes. Scattered over this wide surface, they have up to the present been too separated from one another to feel all the ties which bind them. But by virtue of the very fact that they will push their researches beyond the point of departure, they will of necessity come together with consequent solidarity. Science will thus be unified by its own activities, not by the abstract unity of a formula too inadequate for the multitude of things that it must embrace, but by the living unity of an organic whole. In order to be unified science need not be comprehended by one and the same mind —an impossible task in any case. To achieve that end of unification those who work in it need only feel that they are working together in a common task.

7

The Social Basis of Religion
and the Sociology of Knowledge

Durkheim's systematic concern with religion has personal roots in his family's ties to organized Judaism. His investigations of primitive religion begin early with the Division of Labor in Society, and in Suicide much is made of the Protestant proclivity to self-destruction. His anthropological investigations intensified his interest in the problem of the relation of religion to social organization. In The Elementary Forms of the Religious Life, he finally turns loose this absorbing concern and probes directly and systematically into the social utility of religion, its social origins, and the way in which abstract religious and cosmological concepts reflect social organization. Through the last of these pursuits he opens up the field now called "the sociology of knowledge."

Durkheim views religion as a social fact. It exists and must be recognized by sociology as a social institution. Human beliefs in the supernatural and the sacred are social realities, even if the supernatural and the sacred are not external realities. The aim of sociology is to discover scientific laws concerning the universal phenomenon of religion. The pursuit of this aim, Durkheim holds, is facilitated by studying religious beliefs and practices in primitive societies. He therefore concentrates his large study upon the religious beliefs and practices of the Australian tribes. For this exclusive concentration upon one type of primitive society Durkheim has been called seriously to task.

Durkheim's general conclusion is that religion is eminently social, that religious representations are collective representations expressive of collective realities. Conceptual thinking turns out to be deter-

85

mined by social organization too, according to Durkheim. The concepts of space and time, of class, of force, of personality, and of efficacy—even the principles of contradiction and identity, the basic constructs in formal logic—he finds emanating from collective representations basic in social organization.

In Durkheim, no defense can be found for the contemporary view that religion may first be a reflection of man's own psychic nature and that only its specific elaborations in different times and places are explicable through social organization.

Durkheim's sociology of religion can be used for markedly conservative purposes, though he himself might have disowned them. Collective representations, which are enshrined as beliefs and worshipped in rites, stress the glories of the past. As systematized and organized through churches they may tend to become the means of keeping men subservient to a social organization of benefit only to those who have political and economic power. In modern democratic societies differences among religions are tolerated because of fundamental secular agreements, but conflicts among them can become so grievous as to endanger the delicate balance that Durkheim calls "solidarity."

Utility and Universality of Religion*

. . . There are no religions which are false. All are true in their own fashion; all answer, though in different ways, to the given conditions of human existence. It is undeniably possible to arrange them in a hierarchy. Some can be called superior to others, in the sense that they call into play higher mental functions, that they are richer in ideas and sentiments, that they contain more concepts with fewer sensations and images, and that their arrangement is wiser. But howsoever real this greater complexity and this higher ideality may be, they are not sufficient to place the corresponding religions in different classes. All are religions equally, just as all living beings are equally alive, from the most humble plastids up to man. So when we turn to primitive religions it is not with the idea of depreciating religion in general, for these religions are no less respectable than the others. They respond to the same needs, they play the same rôle, they depend

* From The Elementary Forms of the Religious Life, pp. 3, 5.

upon the same causes; they can also well serve to show the nature of the religious life, and consequently to resolve the problem which we wish to study.

. . . . .

. . . At the foundation of all systems of beliefs and of all cults there ought necessarily to be a certain number of fundamental representations or conceptions and of ritual attitudes which, in spite of the diversity of forms which they have taken, have the same objective significance and fulfil the same functions everywhere. These are the permanent elements which constitute that which is permanent and human in religion; they form all the objective contents of the idea which is expressed when one speaks of religion in general. . . .

Definition of Religion*

. . . A religion is a unified system of beliefs and practices relative to sacred things, that is to say, things set apart and forbidden—beliefs and practices which unite into one single moral community called a Church, all those who adhere to them. The second element which thus finds a place in our definition is no less essential than the first; for by showing that the idea of religion is inseparable from that of the Church, it makes it clear that religion should be an eminently collective thing.

Origin of Religion†

. . . If by origin we are to understand the very first beginning, the question has nothing scientific about it, and should be resolutely discarded. There was no given moment when religion began to exist, and there is consequently no need of finding a means of transporting ourselves thither in thought. Like every human institution, religion did not commence anywhere. Therefore, all speculations of this sort are justly discredited; they can only consist in subjective and arbitrary constructions which are subject to no sort of control. But the prob-

* From *The Elementary Forms of the Religious Life*, p. 47.
† From *The Elementary Forms of the Religious Life*, p. 8.

lem which we raise is quite another one. What we want to do is to find a means of discerning the ever-present causes upon which the most essential forms of religious thought and practice depend. . . . These causes are proportionately more easily observable as the societies where they are observed are less complicated. That is why we try to get as near as possible to the origins.[1] It is not that we ascribe particular virtues to the lower religions. On the contrary, they are rudimentary and gross; we cannot make of them a sort of model which later religions only have to reproduce. But even their grossness makes them instructive, for they thus become convenient for experiments, as in them, the facts and their relations are easily seen. In order to discover the laws of the phenomena which he studies, the physicist tries to simplify these latter and rid them of their secondary characteristics. For that which concerns institutions, nature spontaneously makes the same sort of simplifications at the beginning of history. . . .

Religious Foundations of Logical Thought*

The general conclusion . . . [of The Elementary Forms of the Religious Life] is that religion is something eminently social. Religious representations are collective representations which express collective realities; the rites are a manner of acting which take rise in the midst of the assembled groups and which are destined to excite, maintain or recreate certain mental states in these groups. So if the categories are of religious origin, they ought to participate in this nature common to all religious facts; they too should be social affairs and the product of collective thought. At least—for in the actual condition of our knowledge of these matters, one should be careful to avoid all radical and exclusive statements—it is allowable to suppose that they are rich in social elements.

Even at present, these can be imperfectly seen in some of them.

[1] It is seen that we give a wholly relative sense to this word "origins," just as to the word "primitive." By it we do not mean an absolute beginning, but the most simple social condition that is actually known or that beyond which we cannot go at present. When we speak of the origins or of the commencement of religious history or thought, it is in this sense that our statements should be understood.

* From The Elementary Forms of the Religious Life, pp. 10–13.

For example, try to represent what the notion of time would be without the processes by which we divide it, measure it or express it with objective signs, a time which is not a succession of years, months, weeks, days and hours! This is something nearly unthinkable. We cannot conceive of time, except on condition of distinguishing its different moments. Now what is the origin of this differentiation? Undoubtedly, the states of consciousness which we have already experienced can be reproduced in us in the same order in which they passed in the first place; thus portions of our past become present again, though being clearly distinguished from the present. But howsoever important this distinction may be for our private experience, it is far from being enough to constitute the notion or category of time. This does not consist merely in a commemoration, either partial or integral, of our past life. It is an abstract and impersonal frame which surrounds, not only our individual existence, but that of all humanity. It is like an endless chart, where all duration is spread out before the mind, and upon which all possible events can be located in relation to fixed and determined guide lines. It is not my time that is thus arranged; it is time in general, such as it is objectively thought of by everybody in a single civilization. That alone is enough to give us a hint that such an arrangement ought to be collective. And in reality, observation proves that these indispensable guide lines, in relation to which all things are temporally located, are taken from social life. The divisions into days, weeks, months, years, etc., correspond to the periodical recurrence of rites, feasts, and public ceremonies. A calendar expresses the rhythm of the collective activities, while at the same time its function is to assure their regularity.[2]

It is the same thing with space. As Hamelin has shown, space is not the vague and indetermined medium which Kant imagined; if purely and absolutely homogeneous, it would be of no use, and could not be grasped by the mind. Spatial representation consists essentially

[2] Thus we see all the difference which exists between the group of sensations and images which serve to locate us in time, and the category of time. The first are the summary of individual experiences, which are of value only for the person who experienced them. But what the category of time expresses is a time common to the group, a social time, so to speak. In itself it is a veritable social institution. Also, it is peculiar to man; animals have no representations of this sort.

This distinction between the category of time and the corresponding sensations could be made equally well in regard to space or cause. Perhaps this would aid in clearing up certain confusions which are maintained by the controversies of which these questions are the subject. . . .

in a primary co-ordination of the data of sensuous experience. But this co-ordination would be impossible if the parts of space were qualitatively equivalent and if they were really interchangeable. To dispose things spatially there must be a possibility of placing them differently, of putting some at the right, others at the left, these above, those below, at the north of or at the south of, east or west of, etc., etc., just as to dispose states of consciousness temporally there must be a possibility of localizing them at determined dates. That is to say that space could not be what it is if it were not, like time, divided and differentiated. But whence come these divisions which are so essential? By themselves, there are neither right nor left, up nor down, north nor south, etc. All these distinctions evidently come from the fact that different sympathetic values have been attributed to various regions. Since all the men of a single civilization represent space in the same way, it is clearly necessary that these sympathetic values, and the distinctions which depend upon them, should be equally universal, and that almost necessarily implies that they be of social origin.[3]

Besides that, there are cases where this social character is made manifest. There are societies in Australia and North America where space is conceived in the form of an immense circle, because the camp has a circular form; and this spatial circle is divided up exactly like the tribal circle, and is in its image. There are as many regions distinguished as there are clans in the tribe, and it is the place occupied by the clans inside the encampment which has determined the orientation of these regions. Each region is defined by the totem of the clan to which it is assigned. Among the Zuñi, for example, the pueblo contains seven quarters; each of these is a group of clans which has had a unity: in all probability it was originally a single clan which was later subdivided. Now their space also contains seven quarters, and each of these seven quarters of the world is in intimate connection with a quarter of the pueblo, that is to say with a group of clans.[4]

[3] Or else it would be necessary to admit that all individuals, in virtue of their organo-physical constitution, are spontaneously affected in the same manner by the different parts of space: which is more improbable, especially as in themselves the different regions are sympathetically indifferent. Also, the divisions of space vary with different societies, which is a proof that they are not founded exlcusively upon the congenital nature of man.

[4] See Durkheim and Mauss, De quelques formes primitives de classification, in Année Sociologique, VI, p. 34.

"Thus," says Cushing, "one division is thought to be in relation with the north, another represents the west, another the south," etc.[5] Each quarter of the pueblo has its characteristic colour, which symbolizes it; each region has its colour, which is exactly the same as that of the corresponding quarter. In the course of history the number of fundamental clans has varied; the number of the fundamental regions of space has varied with them. Thus the social organization has been the model for the spatial organization and a reproduction of it. It is thus even up to the distinction between right and left which, far from being inherent in the nature of man in general, is very probably the product of representations which are religious and therefore collective.[6]

Analogous proofs will be found presently in regard to the ideas of class, force, personality and efficacy. It is even possible to ask if the idea of contradiction does not also depend upon social conditions. What makes one tend to believe this is that the empire which the idea has exercised over human thought has varied with times and societies. Today the principle of identity dominates scientific thought; but there are vast systems of representations which have played a considerable rôle in the history of ideas where it has frequently been set aside: these are the mythologies, from the grossest up to the most reasonable.[6] There, we are continually coming upon beings which have the most contradictory attributes simultaneously, who are at the same time one and many, material and spiritual, who can divide themselves up indefinitely without losing anything of their constitution; in mythology it is an axiom that the part is worth the whole. These variations through which the rules which seem to govern our present logic have passed prove that, far from being engraven through all eternity upon the mental constitution of men, they depend, at

[5] Zuñi Creation Myths, in 13th Rep. of the Bureau of Amer. Ethnol., pp. 367ff.
[6] See Hertz, La prééminence de la main droite. Etude de polarité religieuse, in the Revue Philosophique, Dec., 1909. On this same question of the relations between the representation of space and the form of the group, see the chapter in Ratzel, Politische Geographie, entitled Der Raum in Geist der Völker.
[6] We do not mean to say that mythological thought ignores it, but that it contradicts it more frequently and openly than scientific thought does. Inversely, we shall show that science cannot escape violating it, though it holds to it far more scrupulously than religion does. On this subject, as on many others, there are only differences of degree between science and religion; but if these differences should not be exaggerated, they must be noted, for they are significant.

least in part, upon factors that are historical and consequently social.
We do not know exactly what they are, but we may presume that
they exist.

Sociology of Religion and
Sociology of Knowledge*

. . . The problem of knowledge is thus posed in new terms. . . .
The fundamental proposition of the apriorist theory is that knowledge
is made up of two sorts of elements, which cannot be reduced into
one another, and which are like two distinct layers superimposed one
upon the other. Our hypothesis keeps this principle intact. In fact,
that knowledge which is called empirical, the only knowledge of
which the theorists of empiricism have made use in constructing the
reason, is that which is brought into our minds by the direct action
of objects. It is composed of individual states which are completely
explained by the psychical nature of the individual. If, on the other
hand, the categories are, as we believe they are, essentially collective
representations, before all else, they should show the mental states
of the group; they should depend upon the way in which this is
founded and organized, upon its morphology, upon its religious, moral
and economic institutions, etc. So between these two sorts of representations there is all the difference which exists between the individual and the social, and one can no more derive the second from the
first than he can deduce society from the individual, the whole
from the part, the complex from the simple. Society is a reality sui
generis; it has its own peculiar characteristics, which are not found
elsewhere and which are not met with again in the same form in all
the rest of the universe. The representations which express it have
wholly different contents from purely individual ones and we may
rest assured in advance that the first add something to the second.

Even the manner in which the two are formed results in differen-
tiating them. Collective representations are the result of an immense
co-operation, which stretches out not only into space but into time
as well; to make them, a multitude of minds have associated, united
and combined their ideas and sentiments; for them, long generations

* From *The Elementary Forms of the Religious Life*, pp. 13, 15-18, 19-20.

have accumulated their experience and their knowledge. A special intellectual activity is therefore concentrated in them which is infinitely richer and complexer than that of the individual. From that one can understand how the reason has been able to go beyond the limits of empirical knowledge. It does not owe this to any vague mysterious virtue but simply to the fact that according to the well-known formula, man is double. There are two beings in him: an individual being which has its foundation in the organism and the circle of whose activities is therefore strictly limited, and a social being which represents the highest reality in the intellectual and moral order that we can know by observation—I mean society. This duality of our nature has as its consequence in the practical order, the irreducibility of a moral ideal to a utilitarian motive, and in the order of thought, the irreducibility of reason to individual experience. In so far as he belongs to society, the individual transcends himself, both when he thinks and when he acts.

This same social character leads to an understanding of the origin of the necessity of the categories. It is said that an idea is necessary when it imposes itself upon the mind by some sort of virtue of its own, without being accompanied by any proof. It contains within it something which constrains the intelligence and which leads to its acceptance without preliminary examination. The apriorist postulates this singular quality, but does not account for it; for saying that the categories are necessary because they are indispensable to the functioning of the intellect is simply repeating that they are necessary. But if they really have the origin which we attribute to them, their ascendancy no longer has anything surprising in it. They represent the most general relations which exist between things; surpassing all our other ideas in extension, they dominate all the details of our intellectual life. If men did not agree upon these essential ideas at every moment, if they did not have the same conception of time, space, cause, number, etc., all contact between their minds would be impossible, and with that, all life together. Thus society could not abandon the categories to the free choice of the individual without abandoning itself. If it is to live there is not merely need of a satisfactory moral conformity, but also there is a minimum of logical conformity beyond which it cannot safely go. For this reason it uses all its authority upon its members to forestall such dissidences. Does a mind ostensibly free itself from these forms of thought? It is no longer considered a human mind in the full sense of the word, and is treated accordingly. That is why we feel that we are no longer completely free and that something resists, both within and outside ourselves, when we attempt to rid ourselves of these fundamental notions, even in our own conscience. Outside of us there is public opinion which judges us; but more than that, since society is also represented inside of us, it sets itself against these revolutionary fancies, even inside of ourselves; we have the feeling that we cannot abandon them if our whole thought is not to cease being really human. This seems to be the origin of the exceptional authority which is inherent in the reason and which makes us accept its suggestions with confidence. It is the very authority of society,[7] transferring itself to a certain manner of thought which is the indispensable condition of all common action. The necessity with which the categories are imposed upon us is not the effect of simple habits whose yoke we could easily throw off with a little effort; nor is it a physical or metaphysical necessity, since the categories change in different places and times; it is a special sort of moral necessity which is to the intellectual life what moral obligation is to the will.

. . . . .

Thus renovated, the theory of knowledge seems destined to unite the opposing advantages of the two rival theories, without incurring their inconveniences. It keeps all the essential principles of the apriorists; but at the same time it is inspired by that positive spirit which the empiricists have striven to satisfy. It leaves the reason its specific power, but it accounts for it and does so without leaving the world of observable phenomena. It affirms the duality of our intellectual life, but it explains it, and with natural causes. The categories are no longer considered as primary and unanalysable facts, yet they keep a complexity which falsifies any analysis as ready as that with which the empiricists content themselves. They no longer appear as very simple notions which the first comer can very easily arrange from his own personal observations and which the popular imagination has unluckily complicated, but rather they appear as priceless instruments of thought which the human groups have laboriously forged through the centuries and where they have accumulated the best of their intellectual capital. A complete section of the history of humanity is resumed therein. This is equivalent to saying that to suc-

[7] It has frequently been remarked that social disturbances result in multiplying mental disturbances. This is one more proof that logical discipline is a special aspect of social discipline. The first gives way as the second is weakened.

ceed in understanding them and judging them, it is necessary to resort to other means than those which have been in use up to the present. To know what these conceptions which we have not made ourselves are really made of, it does not suffice to interrogate our own consciousnesses; we must look outside of ourselves, it is history that we must observe, there is a whole science which must be formed, a complex science which can advance but slowly and by collective labour, and to which the present work brings some fragmentary contributions in the nature of an attempt. . . .

Society, Conceptual Thought, and Science*

We are now able to see what the part of society in the genesis of logical thought is. This is possible only from the moment when, above the fugitive conceptions which they owe to sensuous experience, men have succeeded in conceiving a whole world of stable ideas, the common ground of all intelligences. In fact, logical thinking is always impersonal thinking, and is also thought *sub specie æternitatis*—as though for all time. Impersonality and stability are the two characteristics of truth. . . . It is under the form of collective thought that impersonal thought is for the first time revealed to humanity; we cannot see by what other way this revelation could have been made. From the mere fact that society exists, there is also, outside of the individual sensations and images, a whole system of representations which enjoy marvellous properties. By means of them, men understand each other and intelligences grasp each other. They have within them a sort of force or moral ascendancy, in virtue of which they impose themselves upon individual minds. Hence the individual at least obscurely takes account of the fact that above his private ideas, there is a world of absolute ideas according to which he must shape his own; he catches a glimpse of a whole intellectual kingdom in which he participates, but which is greater than he. This is the first intuition of the realm of truth. From the moment when he first becomes conscious of these higher ideas, he sets himself to scrutinizing their nature; he asks whence these pre-eminent representations hold their prerogatives and, in so far as he believes that he has dis-

* From *The Elementary Forms of the Religious Life*, pp. 436–39, 445–47.

covered their causes, he undertakes to put these causes into action for himself, in order that he may draw from them by his own force the effects which they produce; that is to say, he attributes to himself the right of making concepts. Thus the faculty of conception has individualized itself. But to understand its origins and function, it must be attached to the social conditions upon which it depends.

. . . The scientifically elaborated and criticized concepts are always in the very slight minority. Also, between them and those which draw all their authority from the fact that they are collective, there are only differences of degree. A collective representation presents guarantees of objectivity by the fact that it is collective: for it is not without sufficient reason that it has been able to generalize and mainain itself with persistence. If it were out of accord with the nature of things, it would never have been able to acquire an extended and prolonged empire over intellects. At bottom, the confidence inspired by scientific concepts is due to the fact that they can be methodically controlled. But a collective representation is necessarily submitted to a control that is repeated indefinitely; the men who accept it verify it by their own experience. Therefore, it could not be wholly inadequate for its subject. It is true that it may express this by means of imperfect symbols; but scientific symbols themselves are never more than approximative. It is precisely this principle which is at the basis of the method which we follow in the study of religious phenomena: we take it as an axiom that religious beliefs, howsoever strange their appearance may be at times, contain a truth which must be discovered.[8]

On the other hand, it is not at all true that concepts, even when constructed according to the rules of science, get their authority uniquely from their objective value. It is not enough that they be true to be believed. If they are not in harmony with the other beliefs and opinions, or, in a word, with the mass of the other collective representations, they will be denied; minds will be closed to them; consequently it will be as though they did not exist. Today it is generally sufficient that they bear the stamp of science to receive a sort of privileged credit, because we have faith in science. But this faith does not differ essentially from religious faith. In the last resort, the value which we attribute to science depends upon the idea which we collectively form of its nature and rôle in life; that is as much as to say that it expresses a state of public opinion. In all social life, in fact,

[8] Thus we see how far it is from being true that a conception lacks objective value merely because it has a social origin.

science rests upon opinion. It is undoubtedly true that this opinion can be taken as the object of a study and a science made of it; this is what sociology principally consists in. But the science of opinion does not make opinions; it can only observe them and make them more conscious of themselves. It is true that by this means it can lead them to change, but science continues to be dependent upon opinion at the very moment when it seems to be making its laws; for, as we have already shown, it is from opinion that it holds the force necessary to act upon opinion.

. . . Since logical thought commences with the concept, it follows that it has always existed; there is no period in history when men have lived in a chronic confusion and contradiction. To be sure, we cannot insist too much upon the different characteristics which logic presents at different periods in history; it develops like the societies themselves. But howsoever real these differences may be, they should not cause us to neglect the similarities, which are no less essential.

. . . . .

. . . It is not at all true that between science on the one hand, and morals and religion on the other, there exists that sort of antinomy which has so frequently been admitted, for the two forms of human activity really come from one and the same source. . . . Impersonal reason is only another name given to collective thought. For this is possible only through a group of individuals; it supposes them, and in their turn, they suppose it, for they can continue to exist only by grouping themselves together. The kingdom of ends and impersonal truths can realize itself only by the co-operation of particular wills, and the reasons for which these participate in it are the same as those for which they co-operate. In a word, there is something impersonal in us because there is something social in all of us, and since social life embraces at once both representations and practices, this impersonality naturally extends to ideas as well as to acts.

Perhaps some will be surprised to see us connect the most elevated forms of thought with society: the cause appears quite humble, in consideration of the value which we attribute to the effect. Between the world of the senses and appetites on the one hand, and that of reason and morals on the other, the distance is so considerable that the second would seem to have been able to add itself to the first only by a creative act. But attributing to society this preponderating rôle in the genesis of our nature is not denying this creation; for society has a creative power which no other observable being can equal. In fact, all creation, if not a mystical operation which escapes science and knowledge, is the product of a synthesis. Now if the synthesis of particular conceptions which take place in each individual consciousness are already and of themselves productive of novelties, how much more efficacious these vast syntheses of complete consciousnesses which make society must be! A society is the most powerful combination of physical and moral forces of which nature offers us an example. Nowhere else is an equal richness of different materials, carried to such a degree of concentration, to be found. Then it is not surprising that a higher life disengages itself which, by reacting upon the elements of which it is the product, raises them to a higher plane of existence and transforms them.

Thus sociology appears destined to open a new way to the science of man. Up to the present, thinkers were placed before this double alternative: either explain the superior and specific faculties of men by connecting them to the inferior forms of his being, the reason to the senses, or the mind to matter, which is equivalent to denying their uniqueness; or else attach them to some super-experimental reality which was postulated, but whose existence could be established by no observation. What put them in this difficulty was the fact that the individual passed as being the finis naturæ—the ultimate creation of nature; it seemed that there was nothing beyond him, or at least nothing that science could touch. But from the moment when it is recognized that above the individual there is society, and that this is not a nominal being created by reason, but a system of active forces, a new manner of explaining men becomes possible. To conserve his distinctive traits it is no longer necessary to put them outside experience. At least, before going to this last extremity, it would be well to see if that which surpasses the individual, though it is within him, does not come from this super-individual reality which we experience in society. To be sure, it cannot be said at present to what point these explanations may be able to reach, and whether or not they are of a nature to resolve all the problems. But it is equally impossible to mark in advance a limit beyond which they cannot go. What must be done is to try the hypothesis and submit it as methodically as possible to the control of facts. This is what we have tried to do.

Sociology and Education

Durkheim's interest in and concern for education date from his earliest teaching days in the lyceums. On his visit to Germany in 1885–86, he made a study of the educational system there. Both of his university teaching posts—at Bordeaux and at Paris—involved work in "the science of education."

In the essays in Education and Sociology Durkheim distinguishes education from pedagogy. Pedagogy concerns the techniques of teaching and accordingly utilizes psychological knowledge both of an individual sort relative to learning theory and practice and of a collective sort relative to the classroom group. Education, on the other hand, is eminently and wholly social in seeking to establish in the young those moral forces which give society its strength. Although contemporary society demands the inculcation in the young of enlightened science, this categorical necessity for Durkheim does not, however, negate the need for specialized education for different occupations and hence for diversification.

"The man whom education should realize in us is not the man such as nature has made him, but as the society wishes him to be; and it wishes him such as its internal economy calls for." The aim and end of education is to instill in the individual those states of collective thinking and canons of morals that express the group or groups of which a man is a part. "These are religious beliefs, moral beliefs and practices, national and occupational traditions, collective opinions of every kind. Their totality forms the social being. To constitute this being in each of us is the end of education." In language more evangelical than realistic Durkheim adds that education "creates in man a new man, and this man is made up of all the best in

99

us, of all that gives value and dignity to life. This creative quality is, moreover, a special prerogative of human education."

In his educational thinking, Durkheim tends toward an error that also mars some of his thinking about the reality of society—the error of hypostasis. That is, he establishes fictional, artifactual substances—"education" and "society"—and treats them like real, integral substances, endowing them with moral powers and applying them as thus hypostatized. Yet, as Durkheim in other places sees clearly, society is made up of social institutions in conflict with each other. Within each separate institution, moreover, there may be internal conflict among the groups involved. In educational practice as elsewhere, "society" is not at work, but interest groups are. Some of these interest groups are concerned not with "general welfare" but with advancing their interests against it as defined by other groups.

Definition of Education
and Its Social Character*

. . . Education is the influence exercised by adult generations on those that are not yet ready for social life. Its object is to arouse and to develop in the child a certain number of physical, intellectual and moral states which are demanded of him by both the political society as a whole and the special milieu for which he is specifically destined.

. . . . .

One sees . . . to what man would be reduced if there were withdrawn from him all that he has derived from society: he would fall to the level of an animal. If he has been able to surpass the stage at which animals have stopped, it is primarily because he is not reduced to the fruit only of his personal efforts, but co-operates regularly with his fellow-creatures; and this makes the activity of each more productive. It is chiefly as a result of this that the products of the work of one generation are not lost for that which follows. Of what an animal has been able to learn in the course of his individual existence, almost nothing can survive him. By contrast, the results of human experience are preserved almost entirely and in detail, thanks to books, sculptures, tools, instruments of every kind that are trans-

* From *Education and Sociology*, pp. 71, 77–78.

mitted from generation to generation, oral tradition, etc. The soil of nature is thus covered with a rich deposit that continues to grow constantly. Instead of dissipating each time that a generation dies out and is replaced by another, human wisdom accumulates without limit, and it is this unlimited accumulation that raises man above the beast and above himself. But, just as in the case of the co-operation which was discussed first, this accumulation is possible only in and through society. For in order that the legacy of each generation may be able to be preserved and added to others, it is necessary that there be a moral personality which lasts beyond the generations that pass, which binds them to one another: it is society. Thus the antagonism that has too often been admitted between society and individual corresponds to nothing in the facts. Indeed, far from these two terms being in opposition and being able to develop only each at the expense of the other, they imply each other. The individual, in willing society, wills himself. The influence that it exerts on him, notably through education, does not at all have as its object and its effect to repress him, to diminish him, to denature him, but, on the contrary, to make him grow and to make of him a truly human being. No doubt, he can grow thus only by making an effort. But this is precisely because this power to put forth voluntary effort is one of the most essential characteristics of man.

Education, Society, and Sociology *

. . . Education, far from having as its unique or principal object the individual and his interests, is above all the means by which society perpetually recreates the conditions of its very existence. Can society survive only if there exists among its members a sufficient homogeneity? Education perpetuates and reinforces this homogeneity by fixing in advance, in the mind of the child, the essential similarities that collective life presupposes. But, on the other hand, without a certain diversity, would all co-operation be impossible? Education assures the persistence of this necessary diversity by becoming itself diversified and by specializing. It consists, then, in one or another of its aspects, of a systematic socialization of the young generation. In each of us, it may be said, there exist two beings which,

* From *Education and Sociology*, pp. 123–24, 126–29.

while inseparable except by abstraction, remain distinct. One is made up of all the mental states which apply only to ourselves and to the events of our personal lives. This is what might be called the individual being. The other is a system of ideas, sentiments, and practices which express in us, not our personality, but the group or different groups of which we are part; these are religious beliefs, moral beliefs and practices, national or ocupational traditions, collective opinions of every kind. Their totality forms the social being. To constitute this being in each of us is the end of education.

It is here, moreover, that are best shown the importance of its role and the fruitfulness of its influence. Indeed, not only is this social being not given, fully formed, in the primitive constitution of man, but it has not resulted from it through a spontaneous development. . . .

. . . . .

A ceremony found in many societies clearly demonstrates this distinctive feature of human education [transmission of ideas, sentiments, and expressions] and shows, too, that man was aware of it very early. It is the initiation ceremony. It takes place when education is completed; generally, too, it brings to a close a last period in which the elders conclude the instruction of the young man by revealing to him the most fundamental beliefs and the most sacred rites of the tribe. Once this is accomplished, the person who has undergone it takes his place in the society; he leaves the women, among whom he had passed his whole childhood; henceforth, his place is among the warriors; at the same time, he becomes conscious of his sex, all the rights and duties of which he assumes from then on. He has become a man and a citizen. Now, it is a belief universally diffused among all these peoples that the initiate, by the very fact of initiation, has become an entirely new man: he changes his personality, he takes another name, and we know that the name was not then considered as a simple verbal sign, but as an essential element of the person. Initiation was considered as a second birth. The primitive mind conceives of this transformation symbolically, imagining that a spiritual principle, a sort of new soul, has come to be incarnated in the individual. But if we separate from this belief the mythical forms in which it is enveloped, do we not find under the symbol this idea, obscurely glimpsed, that education has had the effect of creating a new being in man? It is the social being.

However, it will be said, if one can indeed conceive that the distinctively moral qualities, because they impose privations on the individual, because they inhibit his natural impulses, can be developed in us only under an outside influence, are there not others which every man wishes to acquire and seeks spontaneously? Such are the divers qualities of the intelligence which allow him better to adapt his behavior to the nature of things. Such, too, are the physical qualities and everything that contributes to the vigor and health of the organism. For the former, at least, it seems that education, in developing them, may only assist the development of nature itself, only lead the individual to a state of relative perfection toward which he tends by himself, although he attains it more rapidly thanks to the co-operation of society.

But what demonstrates, despite appearances, that here as elsewhere education answers above all to external, that is social, necessities, is that there are societies in which these qualities have not been cultivated at all, and that in every case they have been understood very differently in different societies. The advantages of a solid intellectual culture have been far from recognized by all peoples. Science and the critical mind, that we rate so high today, were for a long time held in suspicion. Do we not know a great doctrine which proclaims happy the poor in spirit? And we must guard against believing that this indifference to knowledge had been artificially imposed on men in violation of their nature. By themselves, they had then no desire for science, quite simply because the societies of which they were part did not at all feel the need of it. To be able to live they needed, above all, strong and respected traditions. Now, tradition does not arouse, but tends rather to preclude, thought and reflection. It is not otherwise with respect to physical qualities. Where the state of the social milieu inclines the public conscience toward asceticism, physical education will be spontaneously relegated to the background. . . .

. . . . .

You see to what degree psychology by itself is an inadequate resource for the pedagogue. Not only . . . is it society that outlines for the individual the ideal which he should realize through education, but more, in the individual nature there are no determinate tendencies, no defined states which are like a first aspiration to this ideal, which can be regarded as its internal and anticipated form. There is no doubt that there exist in us very general aptitudes without which it would evidently be unrealizable. If man can learn to sacrifice himself, it is because he is not incapable of sacrifice; if he has been able to submit himself to the discipline of science, it is because it was not unsuitable to him. Through the very fact that we are an integral part of the universe, we care about something else than ourselves; there is in us, therefore, a primary impersonality which prepares for disinterestedness. Similarly, by the fact that we think, we have a certain tendency to know. But between these vague and confused predispositions (mixed, besides, with all kinds of contrary predispositions) and the very definite and very particular form that they take under the influence of society, there is an abyss. It is impossible for even the most penetrating analysis to perceive in advance, in these indistinct potentialities, what they are to become once the collectivity has acted upon them. For the latter is not limited to giving them a form that was lacking in them; it adds something to them. It adds to them its own energy, and by that very fact it transforms them and draws from them effects which had not been contained in them in primitive form. Thus, even though the individual mind would no longer have any mystery for us, even though psychology would be a real science, it would not teach the educator about the end that he should pursue. Sociology alone can either help us to understand it, by relating it to the social conditions on which it depends and which it expresses, or help us to discover it when the public conscience, disturbed and uncertain, no longer knows what it should be.

Pedagogy and Psychology*

Only the history of education and of pedagogy allows for the determination of the ends that education should pursue at any given time. But as for the means necessary to the realization of these ends, it is psychology that must be consulted.

Indeed, the pedagogical ideal for a period expresses above all the state of the society in the period under consideration. But in order that this ideal may become a reality, it remains necessary to mold the conscience of the child to it. Now, the conscience has its own laws which one must know to be able to modify them, at least if one wishes to try to avoid the empirical gropings which it is precisely the object of pedagogy to reduce to a minimum. To be able to stimulate

* From *Education and Sociology*, pp. 110–12.

activity to develop in a certain direction, one must also know what its causes are and what their nature is; for it is on this condition that it will be possible to exert the appropriate influence, based on knowledge. Is it a matter, for example, of arousing either patriotism or the sense of humanity? We shall know all the better how to shape the moral sensibility of the pupils in one or the other direction when we shall have more complete and more precise notions about the totality of phenomena that are called tendencies, habits, desires, emotions, etc., of the divers conditions on which they depend, and of the form that they take in the child. According to whether one sees in such tendencies a product of agreeable or disagreeable experiences that the species has been able to have, or on the contrary, a primitive fact prior to the affective states which accompany their functioning, one will have to treat them in very different ways in order to regulate their functioning. Now it is up to psychology, and more specifically, child psychology, to resolve these questions. If it is incompetent to fix the end—since the end varies with social conditions—there is no doubt that it has a useful role to play in the establishment of methods. And since no method can be applied in the same fashion to different children, it is psychology, too, that should help us to cope with the diversity of intelligence and character. We know, unfortunately, that we are still far from the time when it will truly be in a position to satisfy this desideratum.

There is a special form of psychology which has a very particular importance for the pedagogue: it is collective psychology. A class, indeed, is a small society, and it must not be conducted as if it were only a simple agglomeration of subjects independent of one another. Children in class think, feel and behave otherwise than when they are alone. There are produced, in a class, phenomena of contagion, collective demoralization, mutual over-excitement, wholesome effervescence, that one must know how to discern in order to prevent or to combat some and to utilize others. Although this science is still very young, it now includes a certain number of propositions which it is important not to ignore.

9

Sociology and Democracy

In his book Consciousness and Society, a study of the reorientation of European social thought from 1890 to 1930, the intellectual historian H. Stuart Hughes comments about Durkheim's political ideas as follows: "A loyal servant of the French state Durkheim remained throughout his life. Indeed, [among] his reasons for undertaking the study of sociology at all had been 'his desire to contribute to the moral consolidation of the Third Republic.' Almost alone among the major thinkers we have been studying, Durkheim never wavered in his militant advocacy of democratic and humanitarian values. . . . In Durkheim's mind, science reinforced democracy, and democracy science; he was a true child of the Enlightenment."

Durkheim was born under the Second Empire ruled by Louis Bonaparte, and as a boy experienced the crushing defeat of France by Bismarck's Prussia in the Franco-Prussian war. Under the Third Republic that was established after this defeat in 1870, Durkheim was given educational opportunities which he helped to repay in part by fighting the enemies of the Republic throughout the long drawn-out Dreyfus case with its shocking anti-Semitism. But in World War I he was trapped into French chauvinism and Germanophobia by failing to recognize France's partial responsibility for the war that has been rightly called the most unnecessary one in history. From it sprang all sorts of evil consequences for the liberal tradition that Durkheim held so dear.

In his political thought Durkheim is essentially a pluralist. He sees the State as one organ of society, namely its political organization, but there are other types of organization as well. Basic to democracy is a type of communication between the wielders of State power and the rest of society that rests on deliberation and debate on political

106

issues by the people and on open administration of State activities by political officeholders. Under democracy, individualism and individual expression are paramount. The expression of individual autonomy vis-à-vis the State is possible through the non-State social organizations in which the individual participates. The democratic State endowed with legal power represents the opinions of the mass of the people. It is not bound by ancient tradition or hoary custom but by law and a morality expressing the needs and desires of the deliberating electorate.

In modern mass society the individual needs groups through which he may express himself; otherwise he has no means of making his deliberate opinion felt. For Durkheim the political reform necessary to achieve this expression involves the establishment of intermediate groups between the individual and the State, through which the individual can express himself and exert influence on State policy. The main contemporary political evil for Durkheim is the idea that the mass of individuals in a democracy must be in direct contact and communication with the State, without any intermediary. The way to overcome this evil is through representation in deliberative political law-making assemblies by occupational or professional groups. This idea had taken hold of Durkheim and was propounded at the turn of the century in a long preface to the second edition of the Division of Labor in Society. He would never again let go of it. In Professional Ethics and Civic Morals he hammers at it again. "Professional life . . . takes on increasing importance, as labour goes on splitting up into divisions. There is therefore reason to believe that it is this professional life that is destined to form the basis of our political structure." But as we have noted in the introduction to this book (p. 5), Durkheim's attempt to save the individual from bureaucracy through occupational or professional groups cannot but fail of this high purpose, even though it has its uses for lesser purposes. Occupational or professional groups have themselves become bureaucratized, and we have been witnessing in modern mass democratic society the battle of the bureaucracies, while the individual becomes further confounded, confused, and alienated.

Durkheim would have been saddened, one imagines, if he had lived to see the "Corporate State" fashioned on the basis of political representation by occupational or professional groups that was set up by Mussolini in Italy as Fascism's contribution to political reform. This representation in Fascist Italy was merely the façade that concealed the retention of basic economic power by the large landholders and the northern Italian industrialists.

As far as France was concerned, Durkheim was trying to patch up the Third Republic, which, like its republican and imperial predecessors since the Revolution of 1789, suffered from the fact that that revolution had never been completed. Under the Third Republic, the mass of Frenchmen were beset by a relatively obsolescent industrial economy ruled by a select few corporations and an agricultural economy peopled with narrow-visioned, small-minded farmers. The result was that French democracy under the Third Republic lived a borrowed existence—borrowed ideologically from the Enlightenment and practically from rude and crude compromises that hid the irresponsible squabbling among the grasping groups. The freedom of the press—a democratic cornerstone—has always had hard going, even in republican France. World War I strengthened in France a State living off of manipulated opinion. In the 1930's, attempts at basic political reform failed; the popular front governments could never successfully carry through the economic and political reforms necessary to democratic advance because of industrial and business interests that were basically Fascist. The ripe fruit of this final failure of French democracy under the Third Republic was the quick fall of France in 1940 to the Nazis. Today's attempts to regain France's so-called glory are beset by internal pitfalls. Underneath French politics today is the threat of civil war, despite a Gaullist majority in parliament and dictatorial power in the executive. Underneath, the country is seething with internecine strife, and De Gaulle is a mere passing figurehead of imposed rather than what Durkheim would call organic unity. Even a united Western Europe and its Common Market must reckon with the possibility of another French revolution, for the extreme right is a Gaullist stronghold and the Communists have gained rather than lost influence in recent years.

The difficulty with Durkheim's political sociology is that it consists entirely of structural reform and functional integration, derivative from analogies to biology (structural-functional relationships) and to mechanics (the interdependence of parts). As a political ideology, this functionalism plays down the recognition of the dynamics of conflict among groups in modern society. Sometimes Durkheim sounds almost like a political utopian striving for unalloyed harmony. Better political sociology would have come from his pen if, instead of trying "to contribute to the moral consolidation of the Third Republic," he had seen through it. Perhaps he would have if he had lived to see the aftermath of World War I.

Meaning of Democracy*

. . . All that happens in the milieux called political is observed and checked by every one, and the result of this observing and checking and of the reflections they provoke, reacts on the government milieux. By these signs we recognize one of the distinctive features of what is usually called democracy.

. . . . The State is nothing if it is not an organ distinct from the rest of society. If the State is everywhere, it is nowhere. The State comes into existence by a process of concentration that detaches a certain group of individuals from the collective mass. In that group the social thought is subjected to elaboration of a special kind and reaches a very high degree of clarity. Where there is no such concentration and where the social thought remains entirely diffused, it also remains obscure and the distinctive feature of the political society will be lacking. Nevertheless, communications between this especial organ and the other social organs may be either close or less close, either continuous or intermittent. Certainly in this respect there can only be differences of degree. There is no State with such absolute power that those governing will sever all contact with the mass of its subjects. Still, the differences of degree may be of significance, and they increase in the exterior sense with the existence or non-existence of certain institutions intended to establish the contact, or according to the institutions' being either more or less rudimentary or more or less developed in character. . . .

. . . . If we agree to reserve the name democracy for political societies, it must not be applied to tribes without definite form, which so far have no claim to being a State and are not political societies. The difference, then, is quite wide, in spite of apparent likeness. It is true that in both cases—and this gives the likeness—the whole society takes part in public life but they do this in very different ways. The difference lies in the fact that in one case there is a State and in the other there is none.

* From *Professional Ethics and Civic Morals*, pp. 82–84.

. . . Nowadays . . . we do not admit there is anything in public organization lying beyond the arm of the State. In principle, we lay down that everything may for ever remain open to question, that everything may be examined, and that in so far as decisions have to be taken, we are not tied to the past. The State has really a far greater sphere of influence nowadays than in other times, because the sphere of the clear consciousness has widened. All those obscure sentiments which are diffusive by nature, the many habits acquired, resist any change precisely because they are obscure. What cannot be seen is not easily modified. All these states of mind shift, steal away, cannot be grasped, precisely because they are in the shadows. On the other hand, the more the light penetrates the depths of social life, the more can changes be introduced. This is why those of cultivated mind, who are conscious of themselves, can change more easily and more profoundly than those of uncultivated mind. Then there is another feature of democratic societies. They are more malleable and more flexible, and this advantage they owe to the government consciousness, that in widening has come to hold more and more objects. By the same token, resistance is far more sharply defined in societies that have been unorganized from the start, or pseudo-democracies. They have wholly yielded to the yoke of tradition. . . .

Democracy and the Individual
in Modern Society*

. . . . Democracy indeed, as we have defined it, is the political system that conforms best to our present-day notion of the individual. The values we attribute to individual personality make us loth to use it as a mechanism to be wielded from without by the social authority. The personality can be itself only to the degree in which it is a social entity that is autonomous in action. . . .

. . . . To be autonomous means, for the human being, to understand the necessities he has to bow to and accept them with full knowledge of the facts. Nothing that we do can make the laws of things other than they are, but we free ourselves of them in thinking them, that is, in making them ours by thought. This is what gives

* From *Professional Ethics and Civic Morals*, pp. 90–91.

democracy a moral superiority. Because it is a system based on reflection, it allows the citizen to accept the laws of the country with
more intelligence and thus less passively. Because there is a constant
flow of communication between themselves and the State, the State
is for individuals no longer like an exterior force that imparts a wholly
mechanical impetus to them. Owing to constant exchanges between
them and the State, its life becomes linked with theirs, just as their
life does with that of the State.

Democracy and Intermediate Groups *

. . . . Life must circulate without a break in continuity between
the State and individuals and vice versa; but there is no reason whatever why this circulation should not be by way of agencies that are
introduced. By means of this intercalation the State will be more
dependent on itself, the distinction between it and the rest of the
society will be clearer, and by that very fact it will be more capable
of autonomy.

So that our political malaise is due to the same cause as our social
malaise: that is, to the lack of secondary cadres to interpose between
the individual and the State. We have seen that these secondary
groups are essential if the State is not to oppress the individual: they
are also necessary if the State is to be sufficiently free of the individual.
And indeed we can imagine this as suiting both sides; for both have
an interest in the two forces not being in immediate contact although
they must be linked one with the other.

But what are the groups which are to free the State from the
individual? Those able to fulfil this are of two kinds. First, the regional groups. We could imagine, in fact, that the representatives of
the *communes* of one and the same *arrondissement*, perhaps even of
one and the same *département*, might constitute the electoral body
having the duty of electing the members of the political assemblies.
Or professional groups, once set up, might be of use for this task. The
councils with the duty of administering each of these groups would
nominate those who would govern the State. In both cases there
would be continuous communication between the State and its citizens, but no longer direct. Of these two methods of organization,

* From *Professional Ethics and Civic Morals*, pp. 96–97.

one would seem to be more suited to the general orientation of our whole social development. It is quite certain the regional districts have not the same importance as they once had, nor do they any longer play the same vital role. The ties which unite members of the same *commune* or the same *département* are fairly external. They are made and unmade with the greatest ease since the population has become so mobile. There is therefore something rather exterior and artificial about such groups. The permanent groups, those to which the individual devotes his whole life, those for which he has the strongest attachment, are the professional groups. It therefore seems indeed that it is they which may be called upon to become the basis of our political representation as well as of our social structure in the future.

10

Sociology of Morals

From the very beginning of his professional career, Durkheim was preoccupied with establishing and elaborating a science of morals. As a positivist in his early days, he sought to take ethics out of the hands of speculative philosophers and place it upon a foundation of verified knowledge of how man behaved morally in different societies and of how he learned his moral ideals from the society of which he was a member. In the first edition of the Division of Labor in Society, he published a long separate discussion on the science of morals but omitted it from later editions. On the practical side he was early concerned to combat the moral dilletantism that he thought pervaded the intellectuals of France at that time.

Morality, Durkheim tells us, consists of a system of rules of conduct which presupposes society or group life. The society that morality bids us desire, he announced in later years, is not society as it appears to itself but society as it is or is really becoming. It is doubtful, however, that the average man, despite Durkheim's high-minded urging, can pursue a morality based on such prescience and foresight, though Durkheim in a passage in his work on the division of labor seems to protect himself somewhat against such a criticism as follows: ". . . Beyond the world of clear-cut ideas inhabited by scientists, there is a world of indistinct ideas containing tendencies. For desire to impel will it need not be enlightened by science. Unclear presentiments suffice to make men feel that they are lacking something to stimulate ambition, and to lead them simultaneously to perceive where they ought to bend their energies." Yet even among the learned scientists there is conflict over what society really is or what it is really becoming.

Moreover, not all of human emotional life basic to morality is consumed by society or regulated by it, as Durkheim would have us believe. At the core of morality is the unconscious, which is anti-social and indeed resists socialization. There is a permanent conflict between the dynamic instincts and conventional morality or even between the instincts and what may be considered ideal social moral-ity. In his important book, Freud: The Mind of the Moralist, Philip Rieff has written: "Human relations are seen in terms of clashing intentions, which society at best can regulate but can never suppress. Far from being a residual idea left over from his biological training . . . Freud's theory of instinct is the basis for his insight into the painful snare of contradiction in which nature and culture, individual and society, are forever fixed." Durkheim would not accept this "snare of contradiction" as basic and permanent.

Yet Durkheim's attempt to subdue certain basic moral problems gives us, by virtue of his intellectual insights, some of the most fruitful hints for tackling them anew. By thus advancing their further clarifica-tion, he belongs in the very first rank of earlier sociologists.

What Is a Moral Fact? *

What are the distinctive characteristics of a moral fact?

All morality appears to us as a system of rules of conduct. But all techniques are equally ruled by maxims that prescribe the behaviour of the agent in particular circumstances. What then is the difference between moral rules and other rules of technique?

(i) We shall show that moral rules are invested with a special authority by virtue of which they are obeyed simply because they command. . . . Obligation is, then, one of the primary characteristics of the moral rule.

(ii) . . . the notion of duty does not exhaust the concept of moral-ity. It is impossible for us to carry out an act simply because we are ordered to do so and without consideration of its content. For us to become the agents of an act it must interest our sensibility to a certain extent and appear to us as, in some way, desirable. Obligation or duty only expresses one aspect abstracted from morality. A certain

* From *Sociology and Philosophy*, pp. 35–36, 38.

degree of desirability is another characteristic no less important than the first.

．．．．

. . . . The society that morality bids us desire is not the society as it appears to itself, but the society as it is or is really becoming. . . .

. . . It is impossible to desire a morality other than that endorsed by the condition of society at a given time. To desire a morality other than that implied by the nature of society is to deny the latter and, consequently, oneself.

Society as the Goal of Moral Activity *

. . . Society is the end of all moral activity. Now (i) while it transcends the individual it is immanent in him; (ii) it has all the characteristics of a moral authority that imposes respect.

(i) Society transcends the individual's consciousness. It surpasses him materially because it is a result of the coalition of all the individual forces. By itself this material superiority would not be enough. The universe also surpasses the individual materially, but is not on that account called moral. Society is something more than a material power; it is a moral power. It surpasses us physically, materially and morally. Civilization is the result of the co-operation of men in association through successive generations; it is essentially a social product. Society made it, preserves it and transmits it to individuals. Civilization is the assembly of all the things to which we attach the highest price; it is the congregation of the highest human values. Because it is at once the source and the guardian of civilization, the channel by which it reaches us, society appears to be an infinitely richer and higher reality than our own. It is a reality from which everything that matters to us flows. Nevertheless it surpasses us in every way, since we can receive from this storehouse of intellectual and moral riches, of which it is the guardian, at most a few fragments only. The more we advance in time, the more complex and immense does our civilization become, and consequently the more does it transcend the individual consciousness and the smaller does the individual feel in rela-

* From *Sociology and Philosophy*, pp. 54–56.

tion to it. Each of the members of an Australian tribe carries in himself the integrated whole of his civilization, but of our present civilization each one of us can only succeed in integrating a small part.

However small it may be, we do nevertheless always integrate in ourselves a part, and thus while society transcends us it is immanent in us and we feel it as such.

(ii) But at the same time it is a moral authority; this follows from what we have already said. What is a moral authority if not the characteristic which we attribute to a real or ideal being that we conceive of as constituting a moral power superior to our own? The characteristic of all moral authority is that it imposes respect; because of this respect our will defers to its imperatives. Society, then, has all that is necessary for the transference to certain rules of conduct of that same imperative which is distinctive of moral obligation.

Conventional Morality
and Nonconformity*

The individual can free himself partially from the rules of society if he feels the disparity between them and society as it is, and not as it appears to be—that is, if he desires a morality which corresponds to the actual state of the society and not to an outmoded condition. The principle of rebellion is the same as that of conformity. It is the true nature of society that is conformed to when the traditional morality is obeyed, and yet it is also the true nature of society which is being conformed to when the same morality is flouted. . . .

In the sphere of morality, as in the other spheres of nature, individual reason has no particular prestige as such. The only reason for which one can claim the right of intervention, and of rising above historical moral reality in order to reform it, is not my reason nor yours; it is the impersonal human reason, only truly realized in science. In the same way that the natural sciences permit us to manipulate the material with which they deal, so the science of moral facts puts us in a position to order and direct the course of moral life. The intervention of science has as its end, not the substitution of an individual ideal for the collective, but the substitution of an equally

* From *Sociology and Philosophy*, pp. 65–66, 68.

collective ideal which expresses not a particular personality but the collective itself more clearly understood.

. . . . A rebellion against the traditional morality [some] conceive of as a revolt of the individual against the collective, of personal sentiments against collective sentiments. However, what I am opposing to the collective is the collective itself, but more and better aware of itself. If it is argued that this fuller and higher consciousness of itself is only expressed in and through an individual intellect, I reply that society arrives at this fuller consciousness only by science; and science is not an individual; it is a social thing, pre-eminently impersonal.

. . . . .

Of all moral rules those which concern the individual ideal most clearly demonstrate their social origin. The man that we try to be is the man of our times and of our milieu. No doubt each of us in his different way colours this communal ideal with his own individuality, in the same way that each of us practises charity, justice, patriotism, etc., in his own way. However, so far from the ideal being an individual construction, it is that in which the different members of the group communicate; it is that which above all gives them their moral unity. The Roman had his ideal of perfection which was related to the constitution of the Roman city, just as ours is related to the structure of contemporary society. It is a gross illusion to believe that we have freely conceived it in our conscience.

Moral Facts and Professional Ethics*

. . . . Professional ethics find their right place between . . . family morals . . . and civic morals. . . .

. . . . .

. . . . Now there is only one moral power—moral, and hence common to all—which stands above the individual and which can legitimately make laws for him, and that is collective power. To the extent the individual is left to his own devices and freed from all social constraint, he is unfettered too by all moral constraint. It is not possible for professional ethics to escape this fundamental condition of any

* From *Professional Ethics and Civic Morals*, pp. 5, 7. See also pp. 126–27 in this book.

system of morals. Since, then, the society as a whole feels no concern in professional ethics, it is imperative that there be special groups in the society, within which these morals may be evolved, and whose business it is to see they be observed. Such groups are and can only be formed by bringing together individuals of the same profession or professional groups. Furthermore, whilst common morality has the mass of society as its sole sub-stratum and only organ, the organs of professional ethics are manifold. There are as many of these as there are professions; each of these organs—in relation to one another as well as in relation to society as a whole—enjoys a comparative autonomy, since each is alone competent to deal with the relations it is appointed to regulate. And thus the peculiar characteristic of this kind of morals shows up with even greater point than any so far made: we see in it a real decentralization of the moral life. Whilst public opinion, which lies at the base of common morality, is diffused throughout society, without our being able to say exactly that it lies in one place rather than another, the ethics of each profession are localized within a limited region. Thus, centres of a moral life are formed which, although bound up together, are distinct, and the differentiation in function amounts to a kind of moral polymorphism.

Internal States and Collective Norms:

Egoism, Altruism, Anomy *

When we established the nature of altruistic suicide, sufficient examples were given to make it superfluous to describe its characteristic psychological forms at length. They are the opposite of those characterizing egoistic suicide, as different as altruism itself from its opposite. The egoistic suicide is characterized by a general depression, in the form either of melancholic languor or Epicurean indifference. Altruistic suicide, on the contrary, involves a certain expenditure of energy, since its source is a violent emotion. In the case of obligatory suicide, this energy is controlled by the reason and the will. The individual kills himself at the command of his conscience; he submits to an imperative. . . .

* From *Suicide*, pp. 283–87, 323–24.

The same quality reappears in the simpler suicides of primitive man or of the soldier, who kill themselves either for a slight offense to their honor or to prove their courage. The ease with which they are performed is not to be confused with the disillusionment and matter-of-factness of the Epicurean. The disposition to sacrifice one's life is none the less an active tendency even though it is strongly enough embedded to be effected with the ease and spontaneity of instinct. . . .

There is, finally, a third sort of persons who commit suicide, contrasting both with the first variety in that their action is essentially passionate, and with the second because this inspiring passion which dominates their last moment is of a wholly different nature. It is neither enthusiasm, religious, moral or political faith, nor any of the military virtues; it is anger and all the emotions customarily associated with disappointment. . . . We therefore encounter a third psychological form distinct from the preceding two.

This form clearly appears to be involved in the nature of anomic suicide. Unregulated emotions are adjusted neither to one another nor to the conditions they are supposed to meet; they must therefore conflict with one another most painfully. Anomy, whether progressive or regressive, by allowing requirements to exceed appropriate limits, throws open the door to disillusionment and consequently to disappointment. A man abruptly cast down below his accustomed status cannot avoid exasperation at feeling a situation escape him of which he thought himself master, and his exasperation naturally revolts against the cause, whether real or imaginary, to which he attributes his ruin. If he recognizes himself as to blame for the catastrophe, he takes it out on himself; otherwise, on some one else. In the former case there will be only suicide; in the latter, suicide may be preceded by homicide or by some other violent outburst. In both cases the feeling is the same; only its application varies. The individual always attacks himself in an access of anger, whether or not he has previously attacked another. This reversal of all his habits reduces him to a state of acute over-excitation, which necessarily tends to seek solace in acts of destruction. The object upon whom the passions thus aroused are discharged is fundamentally of secondary importance. The accident of circumstances determines their direction.

It is precisely the same whenever, far from falling below his previous status, a person is impelled in the reverse direction, constantly to surpass himself, but without rule or moderation. Sometimes he

misses the goal he thought he could reach, but which was really beyond his powers; his is the suicide of the man misunderstood, very
common in days when no recognized social classification is left. Sometimes, after having temporarily succeeded in satisfying all his desires
and craving for change, he suddenly dashes against an invincible
obstacle, and impatiently renounces an existence thenceforth too
restrictive for him. This is the case of Werther, the turbulent heart
as he calls himself, enamoured of infinity, killing himself from disappointed love, and the case of all artists who, after having drunk
deeply of success, commit suicide because of a chance hiss, a somewhat severe criticism, or because their popularity has begun to wane.

There are yet others who, having no complaint to make of men or
circumstances, automatically weary of a palpably hopeless pursuit,
which only irritates rather than appeases their desires. They then turn
against life in general and accuse it of having deceived them. But the
vain excitement to which they are prey leaves in its wake a sort of
exhaustion which prevents their disappointed passions from display-
ing themselves with a violence equal to that of the preceding cases.
They are wearied, as it were, at the end of a long course, and thus
become incapable of energetic reaction. The person lapses into a sort
of melancholy resembling somewhat that of the intellectual egoist
but without its languorous charm. The dominating note is a more or
less irritated disgust with life. This state of soul was already observed
by Seneca among his contemporaries, together with the suicide resulting from it. . . .

. . . . .

We should add, to be sure, that [the three types of suicide] are not
always found in actual experience in a state of purity and isolation.
They are very often combined with one another, giving rise to com-
posite varieties; characteristics of several types will be united in a
single suicide. The reason for this is that different social causes of
suicide themselves may simultaneously affect the same individual and
impose their combined effects upon him. Thus invalids fall a prey to
deliria of different sorts, involved with one another but all converging
in a single direction so as to cause a single act, despite their different
origins. They mutually re-enforce each other. Thus again, widely
different fevers may coexist in one person and contribute each in its
own way and manner to raising the temperature of the body.

. . . . .

The role of individual factors in the origin of suicide can now be more precisely put. If, in a given moral environment, for example, in the same religious faith or in the same body of troops or in the same occupation, certain individuals are affected and certain others not, this is undoubtedly, in great part, because the formers' mental constitution, as elaborated by nature and events, offers less resistance to the suicidogenetic current. But though these conditions may share in determining the particular persons in whom this current becomes embodied, neither the special qualities nor the intensity of the current depend on these conditions. A given number of suicides is not found annually in a social group just because it contains a given number of neuropathic persons. Neuropathic conditions only cause the suicides to succumb with greater readiness to the current. Whence comes the great difference between the clinician's point of view and the sociologist's. The former confronts exclusively particular cases, isolated from one another. He establishes, very often, that the victim was either nervous or an alcoholic, and explains the act by one or the other of these psychopathic states. In a sense he is right; for if this person rather than his neighbors committed suicide, it is frequently for this reason. But in a general sense this motive does not cause people to kill themselves, nor, *especially, cause a definite number to kill themselves in each society in a definite period of time.* The productive cause of the phenomenon naturally escapes the observer of individuals only; for it lies outside individuals. To discover it, one must raise his point of view above individual suicides and perceive what gives them unity. It will be objected that if enough neurasthenics did not exist, social causes would not produce all their effects. But no society exists in which the various forms of nervous degeneration do not provide suicide with more than the necessary number of candidates. Only certain ones are called, if this manner of speech is permitted. These are the ones who through circumstances have been nearer the pessimistic currents and who consequently have felt their influence more completely.

11

Sociology and Values

There are no things valuable except as men make them so. Durkheim holds that the establishment of what is valuable is not an activity of some extra-empirical part of man but springs from the ideals implanted in men through society. Society is the center of a moral life. From collective living and group activity spring moral ideals of obligation, of duty, and of responsibility. In times of intellectual and moral ferment reformers call upon men to incorporate these ideals more adequately into their lives.

According to Durkheim in his later years, sociology is the science that analyzes and explains how men construct their ideals and establish their values through collective living. "It does not set out to construct ideals, but on the contrary accepts them as given facts, as objects of study, and it tries to analyze and explain them." In his view, every so-called moral crisis involves some breakdown in social values or some failure to establish values in keeping with an ideal appropriate to a new stage of society.

Western thought has emphasized different aspects of man at different stages of social development: first, Political Man as in ancient Greece and Rome; next, Religious Man in the Middle Ages and the Reformation; then, Economic Man with the rise of capitalist society. Durkheim represents the next stage which emphasizes Sociological Man, the stage when men begin to become self-conscious about collective behavior and are able to see the future of their societies as the central social problem. But the era of Sociological Man also marks the beginning of an intellectual tyranny, however unwitting, which transforms man into a servant of an hypostatized entity called "society." He can be saved from this latter-day tyranny as he emerges into the stage of Psychological Man. In the stage of Psychological

Man which has opened up before us, Society is no longer the basic social fact. A psychic universality in man is found to be asserting itself in every social type. Inherent in the human psyche is an opposition to conventional society. Sophistication entails understanding of this opposition and its direction against convention. Society which is mainly conventional everywhere now can be understood not as the unchallenged center of a moral life, as Durkheim would have it, but as the center of a moral life that Psychological Man calls into question. The duty of the sociologist in the contemporary era of Psychological Man is not to enthrone Society but to challenge it, not solely to understand Society but to seek to change it. Thus sociology becomes not merely the science of morality but a morality in itself. That such a view may not be wholly foreign to Durkheim's trend of thought is the highest tribute that Psychological Man can pay to this magistral figure in sociology.

Value Is Made by Society*

If man conceives ideals, and indeed cannot help conceiving and becoming attached to them, it is because he is a social being. Society moves or forces the individual to rise above himself and gives him the means for achieving this. Through the very awareness of itself society forces the individual to transcend himself and to participate in a higher form of life. A society cannot be constituted without creating ideals. These ideals are simply the ideas in terms of which society sees itself and exists at a culminating point in its development. To see society only as an organized body of vital functions is to diminish it, for this body has a soul which is the composition of collective ideals. Ideals are not abstractions, cold intellectual concepts lacking efficient power. They are essentially dynamic, for behind them are the powerful forces of the collective. They are collective forces—that is, natural but at the same time moral forces, comparable to the other forces of the universe. The ideal itself is a force of this nature and therefore subject to scientific investigation. The reason why the ideal can partake of reality is that it derives from it while transcending it. The elements that combine to form the ideal are part of reality, but they are combined in a new manner and the originality of the

* From *Sociology and Philosophy*, pp. 92–93.

method of combination produces the originality of the synthesis itself. Left alone, the individual could never find in himself the material for such a construction. Relying upon his own powers, he could never have the inclination or the ability to surpass himself. His personal experience might enable him to distinguish ends already realized from those to be desired, but the ideal is not simply something which is lacking and desired. It is not simply a future goal to which man aspires; it has its own reality and nature. It is to be thought of rather as looming impersonally above the individual wills that it moves. If it were the product of the individual will, how could it be impersonal? If in answer to this question the impersonal reason of humanity is appealed to, the question is again only shifted and not resolved. This latter impersonality is scarcely different from the first and must itself be accounted for. If minds are at one to this degree, it is, surely, because they derive their homogeneity from a common source and, in fact, participate in a common reason.

Sociology and the Relation between
Value Judgments and Judgments of Reality*

What finally is the relation between value judgments and judgments of reality?

. . . . All judgment is necessarily based upon given fact; even judgments of the future are related materially to the present or to the past. On the other hand, all judgment brings ideals into play. There cannot then be more than one faculty of judgment.

. . . . If all judgments involve ideals we have different species of ideals. The function of some is to express the reality to which they adhere. These are properly called concepts. The function of others is, on the contrary, to transfigure the realities to which they relate, and these are the ideals of value. In the first instance the ideal is a symbol of a thing and makes it an object of understanding. In the second the thing itself symbolizes the ideal and acts as the medium through which the ideal becomes capable of being understood. Naturally the judgments vary according to the ideals involved. Judgments of the

* From *Sociology and Philosophy*, pp. 95–97.

first order are limited to the faithful analysis and representation of reality, while those of the second order express that novel aspect of the object with which it is endowed by the ideal. This aspect is itself real, but not real in the same way that the inherent properties of the object are real. An object may lose its value or gain a different one without changing its nature; only the ideal need change. A value judgment, then, adds to the given fact in a sense, even though what is added has been borrowed from another fact of a different order. Thus the faculty of judgment functions differently according to the circumstances, but these differences do not impair the essential unity of the function.

Positive sociology has been accused of having a fetish for fact and a systematic indifference to the ideal. We can see now the injustice of such an accusation. The principal social phenomena, religion, morality, law, economics and æsthetics, are nothing more than systems of values and hence of ideals. Sociology moves from the beginning in the field of ideals—that is its starting-point and not the gradually attained end of its researches. The ideal is in fact its peculiar field of study. But (and here the qualification 'positive' is perhaps justified if such an adjective were not otiose before the word 'science') sociology cannot deal with the ideal except as a science. It does not set out to construct ideals, but on the contrary accepts them as given facts, as objects of study, and it tries to analyse and explain them. In the faculty of ideation (faculté d'idéal), sociology sees a natural faculty for which conditions and causes can be found for the purpose, if possible, of giving man a greater control of it. The aim is to bring the ideal, in its various forms, into the sphere of nature, with its distinctive attributes unimpaired. If to us, as sociologists, the task does not seem impossible, it is because society itself fulfils all the necessary conditions for presenting an account of these opposing characteristics. Society is also of nature and yet dominates it. Not only do all the forces of the universe converge in society, but they also form a new synthesis which surpasses in richness, complexity and power of action all that went to form it. In a word, society is nature arrived at a higher point in its development, concentrating all its energies to surpass, as it were, itself.

Economic Anomy and Modern Society*

We repeatedly insist . . . upon the state of juridical and moral
anomy in contemporary economic life. Indeed, in economic life professional ethics exist only in rudimentary form. There is a professional
ethic for the lawyer and the judge, the soldier and the priest, etc.
But if we tried to set out even without much precision the current
ideas on what ought to be the relations of employer and employee,
of worker and management, of industrial competitors among themselves and with the public—how vague the statements would be!
Some pointless generalizations about the fidelity and devotion all
sorts of workers owe to their employers, about the moderation with
which employers ought to exercise their economic power, some dis-
taste for every example of exceedingly evident dishonest competition,
for every example of blatant exploitation of the consumer—that is
about all that would be found in the moral conscience of these professions. Moreover, the majority of these principles are devoid of any
legal strength; they are sanctioned not by law but only by opinion.
How indulgent opinion is concerning the fulfillment of these vaguely
put forth obligations is well known. The most reprehensible acts are
so frequently rendered pure by success that the line between the
permitted and the prohibited, between justice and injustice, has become very thin and seems capable of being shifted about arbitrarily
by individuals. Such an imprecise and inconstant morality cannot
become a code for behavior. The upshot has been that this whole
area of collective life is in large part outside the regulating action of
principle.

To this state of anomy must be attributed . . . the incessant, continuous conflicts and the general disorder whose lugubrious picture
is portrayed by economic life. Since nothing restricts these contending
forces and assigns to them obligations that they must fulfill, they
operate at will and batter each other unmercifully in an attempt to
achieve supremacy. Inevitably the stronger finally drive out or sub-
ordinate the weaker. But the vanquished only temporarily resigns
himself to this enforced subordination; he is not content with it and
consequently this process cannot establish stable equilibrium. Truces

* From *Division of Labor in Society*, pp. 1–4.

imposed by violence are always only temporary; they do not bring peace to the spirit. Human passions can be contained only by a moral power they respect. Without the authority of such a moral power the law of the jungle prevails and, open or concealed, there persists a chronic state of war.

Without any doubt at all such anarchy is a morbid phenomenon since it runs contrary to the very purpose of society—the suppression or at least the moderation of war between men by bringing the law of the jungle under the sway of a higher law. . . .

. . . The hitherto unknown development that has occurred in economic activities for about two centuries . . . has brought about the exceptional gravity of this state of anomy especially today. Whereas they formerly played only a secondary role, today they are paramount. We have long since passed the time when economic activities were disdainfully relegated to the lower classes. In the face of these economic activities, military, administrative and religious functions take a back seat. Only scientific functions compete with them for supremacy and even science today has little prestige except as it serves practical life, which in large part means the economic professions. Hence it could be said with some reason that our societies are or tend to be essentially industrial. A type of activity which has assumed such a formidable place throughout the whole of social life can clearly not remain as unregulated as it has been without bringing forth the most serious problems. It becomes preeminently a source of general demoralization. There is a mass of individuals whose life is taken up almost entirely with industrial and commercial pursuits because economic functions today involve the vast majority of citizens. Since this economic environment is but little governed by morality, the greatest part of the existence of these individuals escapes all moral sanctions. Now, for the feeling of duty to be strong within us the very circumstances of our lives must keep it alert. We are not naturally inclined to deny or thwart ourselves. If we are not impelled at every moment to exercise some constraint over ourselves (constraint upon which morality depends), how should we become accustomed to it? If we follow no other rule but that of enlightened self-interest in the occupations which take up most of our lives, how should we take cognizance of objectivity, of self-abnegation, of sacrifice? Hence the absence of any economic regulation cannot fail to engender effects beyond the economic world itself and thus bring in its wake a lowering of public morality.

The Contemporary Moral Dilemma*

Correctly has it been said that morality (and by morality must be understood not merely moral doctrines but customs) has been going through a fundamental crisis. What has already been said can help us to understand the nature and causes of this unhealthy condition. Within a very short time serious changes have occurred in the structure of our societies. They have moved away from the segmental type with a speed and to a degree never before seen in history. Therefore the morality appropriate to this social type has receded but none other has come into being quickly enough to fill the gap left open in our minds. Our faith is disturbed; tradition has lost its sway; individual judgment is not at the beck and call of collective judgment. Yet on the other hand the functions thus torn asunder during the upheaval have not had time to adjust to one another, the new type of life that broke forth in one fell swoop could not be fully organized, and has in particular not been organized so as to satisfy the need for justice so strongly awakened in our hearts. This being so, the cure for the evil is not to be sought in some restoration of traditions and practices which can live only an artificial and fake existence unresponsive to the actual conditions of social life. What is needed is a cessation of this anomy, the discovery of the means for harmonious interaction of organs which continue to undermine themselves through discordant operations, the introduction into their relationships of more justice and hence the progressive breaking down of the surrounding inequities which are the source of the evil. Our failing is therefore not, as has sometimes been contended, of an intellectual sort; it has deeper causes. Our suffering comes about not because we no longer know on which theoretical scheme we should base the morality we have been practicing but because in some of its parts this morality has been shattered beyond repair and because the morality we require is only in process of establishment. Our anxiety does not spring from the criticism of learned scholars bringing about the collapse of the traditional explanation formerly given of our obligations. Consequently it is not a new philosophical system that can ever relieve this anxiety. Rather, since these obligations no longer have a

* From *Division of Labor in Society*, pp. 408–9.

base in reality, a breakdown has occurred which can be repaired only when a new moral discipline comes into being and takes root. In short, our first obligation today is to forge a morality for ourselves. Such a task cannot be worked out in an ivory tower. The morality can come into being only gradually in and of itself, impelled by inherent forces which require it. But what criticism can and must do is set the goal to be reached. That is what we have tried to do.